An Elephant
For Breakfast

An Elephant For Breakfast

Written and illustrated by

Zella

Zella Books, London

646
1000

Zella Books Limited
www.ladyzella.com

This Zella Books paperback edition published 2014

1

First published in paperback by Zella Books 2014
Copyright© Zella Books Limited 2014

Katherine Studholme asserts the moral right to be
identified as the author of this work under the pen name
of Lady Zella Hunter

A catalogue record for this book is
available from the British Library

ISBN 978-0-9928865-0-9

Printed and bound in Great Britain by Lightning Source

For
Sebastian, Charlotte and Matilda

Kenya, Africa

Wist="Wisteria House

Uncle Cosmo + Josephine

Mother + Father (Uncle Rupert Aunt Alicia)

Socrates   Freddie   Tom   Rose

The Pink House

Uncle Crispin
Aunt Lily

Johnny

Lucky

Bella

Wisteria House

The post box at 17 Paradise Road rattled open. A clang. Freddie, Rose and Tom raced down the sweeping staircase, barely glancing at the small pile of letters that had landed on the floor. They pulled open the front door. The pavement was shiny with rainwater. But there was nothing on the doorstep.

'Perhaps Uncle Cosmo has forgotten,' said Rose with a frown as she shut the door. Hope still shone in her blue eyes.

Rose's brother Tom could not resist taking the opportunity to tease her. 'You are right to worry, Rose. It might get lost, or worse: stolen by pirates!'

Every year, at the start of the summer holidays, Uncle Cosmo, who lived in Africa, sent his five nieces and nephews a gigantic parcel. This year it was late.

Tom saw Rose start to bristle, and so continued: 'This box makes a dangerous journey across Africa, up the Suez Canal, all the way across the Mediterranean and then the stormy English Channel to arrive on our doorstep.'

'Stop it, Tom,' said Freddie, looking up from his pile of books. He noticed Rose's disappointment turning to anger.

'You don't annoy me!' she said to Tom, patting him on the head and ruffling his tangle of wild red hair. She knew this irritated him. Even though Tom and Rose were twins, he was still a full head shorter than she was. When she patted his head it reminded him of this. He ducked away, out of her reach, and scowled at her.

'Don't, Rose,' chided Freddie softly, wagging his finger at her.

Freddie was two years older than Rose and Tom, and doted on by everyone. His gentle humour always lightened the fiercest family argument. He was born with an extra chromosome, so his muscles were a little softer than those of his siblings. This meant some things were harder for him, especially speaking clearly, but his family understood everything he said.

'I am watching you!' came the warm voice of the children's mother, Alicia. Despite her being nowhere in sight, Tom and Rose stopped squabbling.

Number 17 Paradise Road was a glorious old house. It was a grey shade of white and a little neglected. But what made it truly magnificent was the old wisteria that arched over the door and trailed a light-purple line of flowers, which hung like great floral bunches of grapes. According to family legend it had been planted when the house was first built almost 250 years ago. It was because of this ancient plant that their home was called 'Wisteria House'.

Socrates, the children's grumpy cat, lived mostly on the windowsill at Wisteria House. He was called Socks for short. But Tom nicknamed him Rat Teaser whenever he arrived home with a mouse clamped between his teeth as a tender offering for the children, whom he considered too feeble to catch their own.

Uncle Cosmo would send only one gift, once a year. The gift had to be shared amongst all the cousins. Over the years, the timing of Uncle Cosmo's gift was predictable, but its contents were always a terrific surprise. The children looked forward to its arrival on the first day of the summer holidays with the same anticipation as for Christmas.

One year an almost life-sized rocking horse had greeted them. Everyone took turns riding it. Father pretended that the horse could bite and kick. He tried to feed it apples all summer, with no success. He gave the horse enormous respect, treating it as part of the family and saying good evening. 'Just in case the horse takes umbrage and gives me a swift kick,' he explained. His antics made the children laugh.

The previous year Uncle Cosmo had sent musical instruments: a primitive flute, drums, bells and a tambourine. The children formed a band with their cousins, Bella and Johnny, and Lucky the dog. They ran around the neighbourhood making a racket. Lucky wore her bells proudly on her collar. The jingle of these bells alternated with her howls of excitement. It all ended in a marvellous cacophony.

The noise was so great that Socrates refused to join in. He slunk off as soon as the jamming session rose to an intolerable pitch. The children decided that the band needed a name. So they searched the dictionary and found the word 'Urbane'. They thought that they would like their band to be considered polished, polite and sophisticated, so they called themselves the Urbane Six.

The children remembered these wonders as they sat by the window in Wisteria House looking out at the street. It was the third day of the summer holidays. It was raining. And where was the box?

The Pink House

'Go away!' muttered Bella, half asleep. Lucky the dog tried again to wake her by licking her feet. Lucky put her head on the pillow and nuzzled into Bella's mass of black, curly hair, which seemed to grow straight upwards. Bella had read late into the night and was exhausted.

On holiday mornings, Lucky was usually the first awake at 1 Paradise Road. It was never clear why, but she liked to wake Bella first. On this fourth morning of the holidays, Lucky's old tricks weren't working. She turned her attention to the abandoned shoes and socks, playing noisily for a while. But it was not until Lucky bounded back to the bed and started to pant in her face, with dog-damp breath, that Bella woke up.

'Oh, Lucky, you have the sweetest morning breath ever,' smiled Bella good-humouredly.

As soon as she was up and dressed, Bella woke her elder brother Johnny, by bouncing on his bed.

'Get up, get up, get out of bed!' she sang into his ear.

'Go away,' Johnny moaned, and tried hard to ignore Bella. He turned and pulled the bedding over his ears, attempting to sleep on.

'The box might be here!' she cried. 'Come on.' She pulled off his covers completely. He groaned, but at least now he was awake.

Johnny was quiet and calm. Bella was loud and

boisterous. She felt proud that she was the only person who could rattle him, and used this skill whenever it was needed. Somehow these differences in temperament did not stop them being the best of friends.

Johnny, Bella and Lucky lived in the first house in Paradise Road. It was pink and an eyesore. It was completely out of place in this London street, with its lovely old trees and elegant brick and delicately painted buildings.

As soon as they had dressed, Johnny, Bella and Lucky left the Pink House to walk down the road towards Wisteria House, as they did most mornings, to find their cousins and plot the day. As they stepped outside, the rain was so heavy that they had to return for their coats.

Meanwhile, back at Wisteria House, there was a knock. The parents glanced up from their morning papers. 'Is that a special delivery, perhaps?' Father pondered. But the children had dashed to open the door even before he finished his sentence.

There it was. A brown wooden box. And it was

enormous. They read its label, which was addressed to The Urbane Six: Johnny, Bella, Lucky, Freddie, Rose and Tom, c/o Wisteria House, 17 Paradise Road, London, United Kingdom.

The Box

Freddie, Rose and Tom were in the hallway of Wisteria House admiring the enormous box. It was a type of wooden packing case that Mother called a tea chest. For hundreds of years this type of wooden box had been used to transport tea around the world from China and India.

There was another loud knock on the door. The children immediately ran. As they opened the door Lucky came bounding in, then stopped on the carpet

18

and shook herself vigorously, sending a spray of doggy water over the children.

'Oh, Lucky, did you have to do that?' asked Rose, who had borne the brunt of the water. The others laughed. It always seemed unfair that it should rain in summer.

Even as Johnny and Bella were hanging their raincoats over the banister and pulling off their shoes, none of the children could take their eyes off the enormous box that was sitting there in the front hall.

'It's just arrived,' said Freddie, grinning.

'We were about to text you and tell you to come over as fast as you could!' said Tom.

'I can't believe it's finally here,' said Bella.

'I know, I know,' said Rose. 'It's only four days late, but I was beginning to get worried . . .'

'. . . about pirates,' interjected Tom in a serious tone, finishing her sentence for her. Tom grinned at Rose. The others laughed.

'Stop!' said Freddie as Rose threw a punch at Tom, but missed. She glowered at him instead. But no one could be cross for long because the box had finally arrived.

'Shall we see what's inside?' said Johnny as he kicked his wet shoes into the corner. 'I can't wait any longer.'

The five children began to drag the box towards the living room. Above the excitement and chatter of their voices, Rose heard her mother's gruff command: 'Lift. LIFT! I don't want THAT box to ruin my floors.' The children worked together, on the count of three, to lift the box. But it was too heavy.

'I know what we need,' declared Tom.

'So do I,' grinned Rose. They raced to the back of the house and returned with a couple of skateboards. Together the children managed to tilt the box and slide the two skateboards underneath.

'Is this better, Aunt Alicia?' smiled Johnny. He could always charm her.

'Yes,' she said, as she took a seat on the couch beside her husband and opened her newspaper, glancing at it but keeping one eye firmly on the children. She did not want deep gouges across the wooden floor from the sharp corners of the box.

Once in the centre of the room, the children care-fully slid the box off the skateboards.

'We need something to get this lid off – it's nailed down,' Tom said.

'Perhaps a hammer?' said Johnny.

'An old screwdriver to lever it up . . .' Rose suggested.

'An old fork would do,' declared Bella, and went to the kitchen to find one. Meanwhile, Freddie and Tom ran to the garden shed to find the toolkit. They came back triumphant but wet, and carrying a battered yellow box.

From the old yellow toolkit they chose a claw hammer and a large rusty screwdriver. Opening the box was half the fun. They took turns with the hammer, screwdriver and a fork. The excitement mounted as they wrenched out nail after nail, each one extracted like a stubborn tooth.

'I wonder what it could be this year!' said Rose. 'Your turn, Tom,' she said, offering her brother the tools.

'Who needs this old fork?' said Tom, instead choosing the screwdriver and an even larger hammer. 'These corner nails are bigger and really awkward to get out,' he said, and then accidentally banged his thumb instead of the screwdriver. 'Ow! You see what I mean! Your turn, Bella.'

'Fork please!' exclaimed Bella. She managed to insert it between the lid and the box and then pressed down with all her weight. The lid did not move; the fork did. It was buckled beyond use. 'Well, that was useless!' said Bella. They all laughed.

'It's very heavy,' said Bella. 'Perhaps it's full of gold and diamonds from the African mines!'

'Heavy, but not *that* heavy,' said Johnny, taking the implements from his sister. 'I think it's a baby elephant that we can climb on. Imagine: an elephant for breakfast. What a distinguished visitor.'

'Unlikely!' said Tom. 'I think a live leopard is crouching in the box, hungry and waiting to leap out and have us for its breakfast!'

'Or a lion!' suggested Freddie.

The children kept working steadily and with great concentration. It was hard work.

Finally Johnny cried, 'I think that might just be the last nail!'

As the lid came off, even Father lowered his newspaper to see what wonderful thing would emerge. Mother stood up to take a peek. She could not help herself exclaiming 'Such pretty paper!' as the children removed masses of shiny blue, purple and pink tissue paper from the top of the box.

'Oh, look,' Mother said. 'How thoughtful! Cosmo has sent his brothers their favourite tea: African Pride.' She pulled out a black tin box and threw it to Father, who caught it deftly in one hand and grinned. Then Mother looked back into the box. 'Oh, and a big packet of fresh coffee for Aunt Lily and me. Great.' She smelled the cloth bag of coffee beans before gazing back at the tea chest.

Underneath the last layers of tissue there were nine rather large brown squares.

'But what is it?' asked Mother.

Inside the Box

It was very hard to get a proper grip on the dark brown squares. They were tightly packed. The children had to tip the box to slide the first square out. As it emerged, it became clear that it was not a square: more of a brown block. It was long, perhaps almost a metre long, and quite heavy. They laid it in the centre of the table between the plates of half-eaten breakfast.

'What do you think it is?' asked Tom.

They all stared at it silently for at least a minute. Even Lucky was dancing around the box, sniffing, and wagging her tail. She looked as if she was about to lick it, when Bella commanded: 'Stop, Lucky! Sit.'

Bella laughed. 'Silly old Lucky must think it's chocolate. She wants to lick it!'

'Mmmph,' said Father, returning his attention to his newspaper. 'I am with Lucky on this one. It's chocolate.' Now only the top of his red hair was visible from behind his paper as he said, 'She really mustn't eat it. Chocolate is poison for dogs.'

'Chocolate!' the children all screamed in unison.

Rose was the first to press her face against the brown block and try to bite it. It was too big. She moved to the edge and managed to gnaw a little off. She then licked it like a wild cat. The others quickly followed, but only for a moment because Father hollered, 'Enough!'

'STOP this minute,' commanded Mother,

horrified. 'You may not eat chocolate like little piggies! Non, NON, non, non!' she added with a French accent. When Mother was cross her accent became stronger. 'You may admire it,' said Mother. 'But first finish your breakfast. It's salmon and eggs and you mustn't waste it. Then, if you still have room, you may eat a little chocolate.'

Over breakfast they could not stop looking at the chocolate. They speculated how long it might take to eat an entire block. Rose thought it was probably a year's supply. Johnny suggested that, between them, they would have all of it finished by the end of the summer holidays. One thing that they all agreed on was that it was the most splendid present yet.

On closer inspection, they estimated that each block was the equivalent of a hundred big chocolate bars, which, multiplied by nine, made nine hundred bars of chocolate! The summer holidays were six weeks long. That was forty-two days, plus two for the last weekend.

'That means', Tom said authoritatively, 'over twenty bars of chocolate every day.'

'Which is more than four large bars of chocolate each!' exclaimed Bella. Never in their lives had they had so much chocolate. It was a stupendous treat. They just could not wait to get their teeth back into it!

Uncle Cosmo

After breakfast Mother insisted that they help clear all the breakfast plates and do the dishes. As Mother was saying goodbye to Father, the children sneaked a large carving knife out of the kitchen to cut the chocolate.

It was hard to carve chunks of chocolate off the big block. Tom suggested that they try the hammer to speed things up. But Freddie had a better idea. He felt a little thrill of excitement as he leaned forward. He licked the log. The intense richness of the cocoa hit his taste buds like a steam train.

With the parents out of the room, and following Freddie's lead, all five faces were stuck to the chocolate log: Rose was licking the side, Tom found a corner to suck and was clamped to that corner, Johnny was trying to bite it and Bella was gouging out small chips of chocolate with her teeth and finger nails, which left small freckles and pockmarks over the surface of the chocolate.

But all too soon Mother returned with her cup of tea. She shouted, 'Zut alors! Stop this minute! Don't you dare.'

They all drew back, looking both guilty and thrilled at the same time. Freddie found the knife. As they began again, slowly breaking off a large number of uneven lumps, they gobbled huge chunks. They noticed it made their cheeks bulge in odd but very satisfying shapes. The children slipped a few pieces into their pockets. It was not as sweet as normal chocolate, but it was utterly delicious. For the first time that day silence reigned at Wisteria House as the cousins tucked into the brown gold.

A little later, when the rain had eased, the children put on their jackets and went out into the garden to play on the rope swing that Uncle Cosmo had constructed three years ago beneath the old walnut tree. They spoke about him and the great chocolate treasure.

'Uncle Cosmo is the best,' said Freddie.

'I agree,' said Tom. 'He is the finest uncle in the world. How kind to send us just what we always wanted.'

'I still wish he were here to tell us stories of Africa and to enjoy this chocolate with us,' said Bella. 'Uncle Cosmo tells the most amazing stories and makes the best animal noises,' she added, trying to imitate his grand hand-flapping gestures and strange animal sounds.

'I could listen to him for hours,' declared Rose.

'I would love to see his shiny bald head again,' said Tom, with his usual dry wit. This made everyone laugh and feel better. Uncle Cosmo had a perfectly round head that shone as though it were polished each morning.

'It feels like the longest time since we saw Uncle Cosmo,' said Rose.

'Not including photos!' Tom added sagely. They often received a bundle of photos of wild animals, odd insects and only occasionally the beaming face of Uncle Cosmo. 'He always looked so happy.'

'It's as if he's found the best place in the world: a place where he belongs,' said Johnny wisely.

None of the children had been to Africa, although their parents had promised they would go one day. Uncle Cosmo only visited them occasionally. When he came, he was laden with gifts and wild stories of animals. The children yearned to go to Africa.

They particularly loved the stories of Uncle Cosmo's farm. He shared his house with a parrot called Wellington and, as his brothers joked, an ark full of other animals.

'Perhaps it's time we went to visit him,' said Johnny. 'We could finally meet Wellington! Let's see if that bird can really talk.'

'If Uncle Cosmo is ever home long enough!' said Bella. 'He is always away from his farm, and seldom at his factory.' The family wondered how he produced anything there as he seemed to spend most of his time exploring the savannah.

'Let's write a thank you letter to Uncle Cosmo,' suggested Tom, and they all went to find pen and paper. They enjoyed writing letters. They wrote because Uncle Cosmo was hopeless at answering the phone or replying to emails, but he was very good at writing letters or postcards in response. Of course the children all started their letters with 'Thank you', but each child had different tales to share with him. He made each one of them feel like his favourite niece or nephew, even though all five of them could not possibly be his favourite.

Once the letters were written, the children asked Mother if they could go and post them to Uncle Cosmo. She said yes, and told them to pick up some sausages and fresh vegetables for dinner.

When they arrived home again Mother asked them to help cook dinner and invited Johnny and Bella to join them. Rose peeled potatoes, Freddie fried the sausages, Tom trimmed the ends of the beans and broke the broccoli into little trees, while Johnny washed and sliced carrots. Bella skinned the onions and fried them. When Johnny had finished slicing the carrots, he helped Rose to peel the potatoes – these always took the longest to prepare. Later, after they were cooked, he and Rose would take turns mashing them. It was the best job: using the potato masher and then creaming it all together with butter, milk, salt and pepper. It was hard to do the quick little circles with the fork, as Father had shown them, without their arms hurting. Father would wax lyrical over dinner about the mashed potato, refusing to believe that any of the children had prepared it. They loved the praise and even more the pretence that they were still too young to make such lovely food.

'Shall we make dessert?' asked Tom. The others heartily agreed. They all helped make his famous banana ice cream, a recipe that he had invented when he was only eight years old: one banana per person, a good dollop of cocoa and a little milk. Everyone loved it, and Tom thought it was the best ice cream in the world.

'Let's add some chocolate chunks,' suggested Johnny. Bella flung some chocolate into the mixture, which they then spooned into ice cream cones and put in the freezer. Once the ice cream was properly frozen, Tom melted a huge pot of chocolate, as a special treat, and then poured it into a large bowl. The children watched Tom as he carefully dipped the ice creams in the chocolate and put them back in the freezer, and then Rose had an idea. She looked at Freddie and they giggled. Rose put her finger into the bowl and licked the warm chocolate. Then Johnny and Bella did the same. But Freddie, who went next, put his whole hand into the bowl and then started licking his hand, finger by finger. Tom joined them and, not to be outdone, stuck his whole head in the bowl. Everyone laughed. He was so absorbed by the glorious smell and taste you only get when you are head-first in a bowl of chocolate that he did not hear the footsteps of his mother.

'Quoi!' Mother squawked sharply. 'Where are your manners? Tom and Freddie – that's just not civilised! Freddie, go and wash your hands. And

Tom, go upstairs now and take a good hard look at yourself and clean up your act – that chocolate is everywhere.'

Tom was covered: there was chocolate on his chin, round his lips and stuck to his shaggy red locks of hair.

At dinner, Tom said to Father, 'Tell us the story about the hippopotamus!' They all loved hearing about Uncle Cosmo, Father and Uncle Crispin's childhood in Tanzania and Kenya. Their favourite story involved their grandfather trying to take a photograph of a hippopotamus. The children's grandfather was a tall, lean Scotsman.

'Well, the only red thing in view was Grandfather's flaming hair,' said Father. Father, Tom and Rose had all inherited his red hair. 'He had set up his tripod and camera carefully beside a watering hole. We sat in the jeep, watching. The hippopotamus was in the water, mostly submerged. Not much of a picture, really. The hippopotamus did nothing, as hippos do. We waited and waited. It was hot, and must have been hotter in the sun. Finally, your grandfather was so tired of waiting that he started to wave his hands. He hoped the hippopotamus would move or do something interesting: at least more interesting than being mostly submerged in water. Again nothing. Now, being quite a good cricketer, he had a blinding flash of inspiration. He picked up a clod of earth and threw it at the hippopotamus. It landed a perfect six, on its great flat nose. He waved his hands again and peered through the lens . . . What a delight, the hippopotamus was now moving. Click, click, click.

'The hippopotamus left the pool of water in an awkward slow-motion amble and then started to run. It ran fast, and faster. Your grandfather was photographing like a madman. But the hippopotamus was running towards him. Suddenly he grasped the seriousness of the situation. He turned and fled towards the jeep. We had never seen him move so quickly. He did not even have time to collect his camera and tripod. It was not clear if he would outrun the hippopotamus, as they are fairly fast creatures once they get going. The hippopotamus smashed straight through the tripod and camera, and was charging towards the jeep. Our driver had turned the engine on already. As he leapt in, the driver flattened the accelerator to the floor. Then we drove like mad to escape the furious hippopotamus.'

Father told several more stories, and even though the children begged for more, the hour was late and he said it was time for bed. Johnny and Bella had to go home too. But before they did, they needed to decide who should look after the parcel.

'Uncle Cosmo sent it here,' said Rose.

'But I think that it's only fair if we split it,' suggested Tom.

'That's boring!' said Freddie with a cheeky grin.

'Yes,' agreed Bella. 'Let's toss a coin to decide who is the guardian of this brown gold!'

'So do you want to split it or toss for it?' Father asked.

'Toss for it!' they all cried.

'Best of three, then,' said Father. Bella won the first toss, Rose the second and Johnny the third. 'Looks as if we need to take it to your house,' Father said, looking at Johnny and Bella. He helped the children put the box back on the skateboards and they rolled it to the Pink House at 1 Paradise Road.

When the children said goodnight, they agreed that they would meet at Johnny and Bella's house the next morning and, if it was fine, perhaps play some tennis or go swimming. They were tired, but felt excited about the prospect of another day of summer holidays.

The Secret

'He's behind you!' said Uncle Cosmo. His voice was smooth and velvety, like chocolate. His eyes twinkled with mischief. Josephine turned to look. She let out a little involuntary scream. Only inches away, on the other side of the kitchen window, was the pressed-up nose of a baboon. Josephine could just see, past the mango trees guarding the driveway, a further seven pink-bottomed visitors. They were making off with the bread, breakfast cereals and fresh fruit from the outside table. She heard Cosmo roar with laughter.

The baboon at the window let out a shrill cry and ran after the others. Their pace, too, seemed to quicken, as the baboons disappeared in a cloud of dust, and a squabble of noise, down the long dirt road.

'Let's take breakfast inside this morning,' suggested Uncle Cosmo.

Josephine smiled. 'Yes, whatever remains.' They looked outside; the only thing the baboons had left was a vase of fresh flowers. 'We might have to eat cake!'

Uncle Cosmo and Josephine cut two thick slices of ginger loaf and poured a strong cup of tea. Together they sat at the dining table, beside the terrace overlooking the garden.

'Your brothers are so lucky to live in the same London street,' Josephine remarked. 'I think having your cousins nearby is every child's dream.'

'Even so, I wonder how they could give up all this,' he said, indicating the great row of mango trees stretching into the distance, and the huge horizons that surrounded them. He added, 'I would miss the heat and the colour of the sky in Kenya.'

'They have blue sky in London too,' smiled Josephine.

'But it's often grey, like concrete. Besides, there just seems to be much more sky here,' said Uncle Cosmo.

'Beneath that concrete-coloured sky of London are some of the finest museums and art galleries in the world,' said Josephine, glowing warmly.

'The one thing I could never live without is this smell,' said Uncle Cosmo, taking a deep breath of Kenyan air. The scents of hot grasses and warm earth floated in through the open window and mingled with that of the freshly cut roses on the windowsill.

Josephine knew that, to Cosmo, this was the smell of home.

'I wasn't born here, like you,' said Josephine. 'I've always missed London. I was only eight years old when we moved to Africa, although after twenty-five years it does feel like home!' She smiled at Uncle Cosmo and then said, 'But when shall we tell your family our secret?'

The Nut

Freddie, Rose and Tom were very happy to arrive at the Pink House just in time for breakfast. Not by chance. Their Aunt Lily made the greatest holiday breakfasts. She had grown up on a sheep farm in New Zealand. Aunt Lily was half Maori and half Pakeha. The Maori are the indigenous people of New Zealand and the Pakeha are the settlers who came later.

Aunt Lily sometimes said, 'You children need a decent breakfast.' Whenever she said this, Bella and Johnny would send the cousins a coded text message – 'Lamb chop' – to alert them to come for breakfast.

Often she would make pancakes, fresh fruit

and yogurt. But occasionally, like this morning, it would be the full shearers' breakfast. This would include lamb chops, lamb's liver, sausages and grilled tomatoes. On the farm, this is was what they had eaten when the shearers came. It sustained them through a long day in the smelly shearing shed.

The children wolfed down this hearty feast (except the lamb's liver). Lucky had been waiting patiently under the table and occasionally growling quietly with anticipation. When they had finished eating, they slipped her some meaty treats.

Then the children looked at each other. There was a moment of silent anticipation.

'Whose turn is it to chop the chocolate?' asked Johnny.

'It's my turn,' said Rose.

Three massive chunks fell onto the table. As she chopped a fourth time, the knife struck something hard. It stopped. Rose tried again. She could not get the knife all the way through. She began breaking off smaller chunks. Slowly, piece by piece, the end of a white nut began to appear. As Rose broke more pieces off she thought the nut looked strange. It did not seem to end and was getter wider, not smaller.

Rose called to the others: 'Come here! Look at this strange nut.' They all took turns to chop more chocolate. Soon they had a massive bowl of chocolate, but no end to the nut.

'Look, it's the size of my hand,' Tom said.

They called Bella and Johnny's father, Uncle Crispin. Uncle Crispin was neither dark nor fair, but bronzed with golden curly hair. He had no idea what this hard white material was. He called his wife: 'Lily, please come and give us your opinion.'

Aunt Lily looked at it. 'It's not a nut that I have ever seen before.' She was mystified.

Uncle Crispin chopped more and more chocolate off, but still the strange nut had no end. It seemed to be getting bigger. After some time, a shape as long as their school rulers was sticking out. It curved slightly and was thin at one end, and then much thicker at the other.

'How long do you think it is?' asked Rose.

'I don't know,' said Aunt Lily.

'If it's not a nut, what is it?' asked Bella.

'I've no idea,' said her father.

Uncle Crispin then telephoned his brother Rupert, the father of Freddie, Rose and Tom. 'You might want to pop in here on your way to work. There is something odd in this chocolate, and I can't for the life of me work out what it could be.'

When Father appeared at the door they showed him the strange white thing, smeared with chocolate, which was poking out of the chocolate block.

Father's face paled. 'Good lord, Crispin, I think it's a tooth.'

Uncle Crispin laughed. 'A tooth? Nothing has teeth that size, even in Africa! And the dinosaurs are extinct. Stop kidding, Rupert!'

Father didn't laugh. 'Elephants have tusks. That looks like the end of a dirty ivory tusk sticking out of the chocolate.'

Now that he had mentioned ivory, the cousins thought that was exactly what the nut looked like. Uncle Crispin picked up the great chocolate log and went to the kitchen. There he washed the chocolate off the tusk. He laid it back on the table. They all stood and looked at the creamy-white protrusion again. They had not the slightest doubt that here was a great ivory tusk, on the dining table of the Pink House, and now only half-encased in chocolate.

After a few minutes Uncle Crispin took his brother by the arm and walked away. He lowered his voice: 'Rupert, this has very serious consequences for Cosmo. Trading ivory is illegal.'

'But Crispin, surely Cosmo would not have anything to do with ivory exports. And he certainly wouldn't send it to our children!' replied Father.

'Perhaps the shipments got muddled and he sent our children the wrong box,' suggested Uncle Crispin. 'You just need to look at the label. It has to be Cosmo that sent it.'

'But Cosmo doesn't believe in that! He wouldn't allow elephants to be slaughtered,' retorted Father, his voice rising slightly.

'Rupert, we don't know that. People change. We've been gone a long time. Perhaps he does this now to make money.'

'I don't believe it!' said Father, dismayed at the thought. But Uncle Crispin had sown the seeds of doubt in his mind. Father looked at the box again. It had clearly been sent by Uncle Cosmo: he had even thought to include their favourite tea and coffee, remembered Father.

Rose went to her father. Looking up at him she asked, 'Is it very bad to export ivory?'

'Yes,' said Father, 'and very illegal. It has been banned since 1989. There was an important convention to protect endangered species, and at this convention many countries agreed to ban the export or import of ivory. Uncle Cosmo could go to prison for a very long time if he's caught trading ivory.'

'Can we help him?' asked Freddie.

'Should we tell the police?' said Bella.

'Or ask him if it is true?' said Tom.

'Or see if there are any more tusks in the rest of the chocolate,' suggested Johnny.

'And can we still eat the chocolate?' pleaded Rose.

Beware the Blackbird

Father looked at Uncle Crispin. 'I suppose eating the chocolate can't hurt,' said Father.

But Uncle Crispin was cautious. 'I am not so sure. It is now part of the evidence against whoever is transporting this ivory. I think that we need to proceed carefully. First, let's put the chocolate out of reach – so our little mice don't nibble at the evidence. Then we should try to contact Cosmo to find out what he sent the children. And after that we must hand the ivory and chocolate over to the police.'

What a day! The children did not feel like playing tennis or swimming. They were worried about Cosmo. He might go to jail. They all felt certain that he was not the sort of person who would take part in slaughtering elephants and exporting ivory. But how had he become involved in such a business? The label on the package was clearly addressed to the children and all the details were correct.

The children studied the packaging again. A tea chest. They knew that his factory still used tea chests. The label was handwritten. Tom thought that it looked exactly like Uncle Cosmo's handwriting.

That evening, back at Wisteria House, no one was hungry at dinnertime, even though Mother had made shepherd's pie and peas, usually a firm favourite with Freddie, Rose and Tom. They looked at each other for long, silent periods. Their mother and father exchanged hot words from opposite ends of the table.

'Cosmo would never touch an elephant, let alone be involved in the export of ivory,' Mother scolded. 'Rupert, how could you even think such a thing about your own brother?'

'People change,' said Father, reflecting what Uncle Crispin had said earlier.

'Not so fundamentally!' chided Mother.

'Cosmo has lived in Africa a long time. Perhaps times are hard. Has he taken the easy option?' suggested Father.

'Don't be ridiculous!' said Mother.

'It's just a possibility suggested by Crispin.' Father was now defensive. 'None of us is perfect. Perhaps his principles have slipped.'

Mother replied, 'No, you must not even think such negative things. It's Cosmo. I refuse to believe it. We must take the ivory to the police and let them deal with it. Cosmo would never be involved in cruelty to animals.'

A heavy silence hung over the table.

Tom asked, 'Have you spoken to Uncle Cosmo yet?'

'No, his secretary said that he's away for a few days. She could not even tell me where he was. She sounded . . .' Father pressed his lips together.

'What?' asked Freddie.

'She sounded a little . . . I can't be sure, but she sounded frightened. She also said something slightly odd that didn't make sense . . .'

Father was momentarily lost in thought.

'What, what, what?' the children implored him.

'She seemed to whisper something. It was strange, it sounded like "Beware the Blackbird". Her voice wavered and then the phone line was cut off,' replied Father.

'Okay, your father and I need to speak to Uncle Crispin and Aunt Lily about this. We want to be sure we make the right decision. Tom, it's your turn to do the dishes. We'll be back soon,' said Mother. And with that their parents left to walk down the street to the Pink House at 1 Paradise Road.

Freddie, Rose and Tom cleared the table and Tom did the dishes. It was beginning to get dark outside and rain rolled down the windowpane like quiet tears. Rose said, 'I feel very worried about Uncle Cosmo. Where do you suppose he could be?'

Just then the kitchen door rattled. A pause. There was another sound. A short, urgent knock.

The children went together to the kitchen door, which faced the back garden, and peered through the glass.

There in the garden stood a bedraggled man, with a long wet coat and a red nose. It took them a moment to realise who it was.

They opened the door.

'Hide me!' whispered Uncle Cosmo.

The Police

The children pulled Uncle Cosmo inside and shut the door quickly. Then they threw themselves on him and hugged him.

'What are you doing here?' asked Rose.

Uncle Cosmo pulled back. 'I must hide. Where is the most secret place you know?'

'Perhaps our cellar?' said Rose.

'Under my bed?' suggested Freddie.

'No, not here. These people have guns,' said Uncle Cosmo.

'The boarded-up house at the end of the street?' said Tom.

'Yes, the abandoned house. That sounds promising. What number is it?'

'Fifty-two.'

As suddenly as Uncle Cosmo had appeared, he disappeared back into the twilight of the garden. There was not even time to ask him about the chocolate. It was the first time they had ever heard urgency in his voice. It told them that he was in real trouble.

Rose had just started to say 'I hope he's okay', when the doorbell rang.

At least their parents were back, the children thought as they ran to the door. But when they opened it, two policemen were standing there.

'Good evening, children. We are looking for your uncle, Mr Cosmo Baker. Are you aware of his whereabouts?'

The children looked at each other, and then at the officers. There was a pause. 'No,' they said in unison.

'Shame. Mind if we come in?' The officers didn't wait for them to answer. They stepped inside.

'You receive any packages from your Uncle Cosmo lately?' asked one of the officers. His tone had become sharper. The buttons were straining on his uniform. Freddie saw that he had grown too big for it. Near his collar Rose noticed his name stitched in silver: PC Adam Strong. The other officer was tall and lean. The name PC Paul Everest was stitched near his collar. He had already put his head around the doors and looked into each of the rooms.

'He usually sends us one every year. But we haven't received one this year. Would you like to see what he sent us last year?' Tom said, trying to distract them.

'Yes,' said PC Strong.

But PC Everest gave PC Strong a withering look and said, 'No, don't bother. We're only interested in any packages received in the last two weeks.'

'Why?' asked Rose, as innocently as she could.

She felt nervous. She watched the tall, thin officer walk into the kitchen. He appeared to be sniffing the air near the kitchen door, the very same door Uncle Cosmo had stepped through moments earlier.

'It's a serious business,' said PC Everest mysteriously. 'Here's my card.' He handed a white business card to Tom. 'When the package arrives, ring us immediately. Don't open it. What I can tell you is that the package could be dangerous. Might be booby-trapped. We'll get the bomb squad round. So don't even try to open it yourselves.'

'Yes,' the children all said, and with that the two policemen left.

The children ran upstairs and peeped out of their parents' bedroom window. The two policemen continued on their way down the street, in the direction of 52 Paradise Road.

Number 52 Paradise Road had once been a grand old house – the finest house in the street. But now it was in a poor state, and had been boarded up for many years. The roof leaked and it smelled of mildew. The latch on the back door was broken, and the children had explored the entire house. The furniture was covered with dust sheets, and there were more spiders and dusty cobwebs than blades of grass in its overgrown garden. The children had spent many happy hours playing hide and seek inside. It had provided a sanctuary from homework and chores. Now they felt a rising level of dread as they thought of Uncle Cosmo hiding in its shadows.

'Do you suppose Uncle Cosmo is in trouble with the law?' asked Rose.

'Yes,' said Freddie.

'They must know that he has smuggled ivory!' said Rose.

'Oh yes,' Tom said. 'I think that they know. But I don't think those two were policemen!'

The Card

'Tom, why ever not?' cried Rose.

'The tall one's uniform didn't fit properly. Did you notice that the legs of his trousers were too short, and the collar on his shirt was a little tight?' asked Tom.

'No,' said Rose. But Freddie nodded.

'I noticed his name badge was Paul Everest,' added Rose. 'And the other shorter, squatter policeman was Adam Strong'.

'The fat one. His uniform was a size too small.' said Tom. 'Also, I don't think policemen come inside your house without being invited, or at least having a search warrant. And look at the business card he gave us. It looks as if it has been printed from a home computer!'

'And look!' said Freddie pointing at the card.

'What?' asked Rose and Tom.

'No police badge,' said Freddie.

'Freddie's right: it doesn't have the police crest on it. And do you remember that they suggested the package might contain explosives? Yet we all know that is complete rubbish,' added Tom.

'How can we help Uncle Cosmo?' asked Freddie.

'I don't know,' Tom replied. 'But we do need to be careful, because if those two are not real policemen then I think they'll come back to search for the chocolate.'

'My guess', said Rose, 'is that they want the ivory, and they are looking for Uncle Cosmo in order to find it. It's lucky then that the box is at Uncle Crispin's house!'

'That's a good point, Rose,' said Tom. 'But if they know us, they may know that Uncle Crispin also lives in this street.'

'Surely they'd have turned the other way towards Uncle Crispin's house if they'd known he lived here?' suggested Rose. 'I think that they know about us because the package is addressed to us at Seventeen Paradise Road. But it will not take them long to work out that Uncle Crispin lives in this street too.'

They heard the front bell ring. The children jumped. It gave them such a fright. Who could it be this time?

Cautiously, they went downstairs to the front door and looked through the hatch. There stood their parents, smiling. They opened the door.

'Haven't you finished the washing up yet? I'll help you!' offered Father.

As they did the dishes the children explained what had just happened. Father asked to see the policeman's card. He agreed that it looked like a fake. But then he took a closer look.

'This is a Kenyan telephone number. Wait a minute: I think I recognise that number. I am sure I do. Let's check. Yes, it's the phone number for Uncle Cosmo's factory. How odd!' He frowned. 'So he or someone in his factory knows about the ivory. But I wonder who?'

Mother said, 'And Cosmo? How did he look? Had he eaten? Was he well?'

Freddie said, 'He looked awful!'

'Yes,' added Rose. 'He looked as if he hadn't slept properly in days!'

'Oh dear,' said Mother. 'I'd better take him a warm supper.' And she began to heat up some of the shepherd's pie, and make a little basket for him. She added grapes, fresh lemonade and homemade chocolate brownies with great daubs of caramel, extra lumps of chocolate, and a little flaky sea salt on the top. For the last few days her brownies had been exceptionally good. She even remembered to take a candle and matches because there would be no electricity in the abandoned house.

The Empty House

'Yoo-hoo,' Mother called into the dark, empty house. 'Anybody at home?' Number 52 Paradise Road appeared deserted.

She put the basket on the kitchen table. As she lit the candle, there were gentle steps behind her. There was Uncle Cosmo. In the dim candlelight Mother thought he looked like a haunted man. She gave him a hug and said, 'Oh, Cosmo, are you okay?'

'Better than can be expected, I suppose. But you run a great risk bringing me this basket of food, although I do appreciate it. Thank you.'

'Don't be silly,' said Mother. 'It wasn't a problem. I only had to cross the road and walk down the street a little way.'

Uncle Cosmo whispered, 'I think I'm being followed. If I'm right, these are very dangerous men. I left Africa in such a hurry: a gun being pointed at me. I've never been more frightened in my life. I was in my car and about to leave work for the day. I was saying goodbye to my secretary, Doris, when to my surprise she gave me a brown envelope. She was explaining that she had booked an open ticket to London, and had made a travel pack with cash, passport and an itinerary. She warned me that I was in grave danger. She was in the middle of saying that she had "overheard two men talking" when she was interrupted. A gunman seemed to appear out of nowhere, and then another was running from the direction of the factory. She screamed and then yelled, "Drive!" I drove to the airport and arrived just in time to catch a plane for London. I was lucky. But I am worried about Doris. I don't know if it was the right thing to run. Perhaps I should have stayed.'

Uncle Cosmo paused and seemed to reflect on his actions. Then he continued, 'When I arrived here I tried to ring her, and she seemed okay, but then the line was cut off before we could speak properly. I think her awful uncle might have arrived – Sir Reginald Ashurst. I find him pompous. But he redeems himself by being entirely devoted to Doris. I will try her again later when he is not around. I've heard of these things happening in Kenya, but I never thought it would happen to me. And in my own factory!'

Mother said, 'Do you think that they want the ivory?'

'IVORY?' he shouted with surprise. Then he added in a low voice, 'What ivory do you mean, Alicia?'

'The ivory tusks hidden in the chocolate bars you sent,' said Mother.

'What do you mean?' asked Uncle Cosmo.

Mother explained, 'When the children first opened your chest no one could work out what it was. Then Lucky helped us guess that it was the most whopping chocolate bars ever!'

'Yes, weren't they an incredible size?' smiled Uncle Cosmo. 'I wanted to send them the biggest chocolate bars in the world.'

'Yes, they were a marvel,' said Mother. 'But there was something else in the chocolate. At first we all thought it was an exotic nut. But, as we chopped into it, the nut grew bigger. Once we had carved off a large quantity of chocolate we found a white tusk in the middle of it.'

'But I sent only chocolate. I sell cocoa and coffee,' said Uncle Cosmo, appalled. 'I don't sell ivory!'

'I know,' said Mother.

'Who could have done this?' asked Uncle Cosmo, almost to himself. Then he seemed to answer his own question: 'I just don't know.' He looked at

Mother and asked, 'And why would anyone do it?'

'I think we both know why,' said Mother. 'There's a lot of money in ivory.'

'Yes,' agreed Uncle Cosmo. 'I have heard such rumours.'

'Perhaps it could be someone in your factory?' asked Mother. 'Who made the chocolate bars for you?'

'In my factory? But I know them like a family. We all work hard. I don't think it could be anyone in my factory.'

'It must be hard to believe,' said Mother, 'but someone in your factory must know how this ivory was hidden in the chocolate.' Uncle Cosmo looked upset. Mother put her arm on his shoulder and continued, 'We are all just glad you're safe and well. Are you sure you don't want to come to our house? We could make you much more comfortable.'

'Alicia, that's very kind. But I'm safer here. And you're safer if I'm here. Whoever did this is very determined; but at least now I know what they were after.'

'Yes,' said Mother, remembering. 'We've had a visit from two men who claimed to be policemen, but they gave the children a card and it had your number on it.'

Uncle Cosmo's eyebrows flew upwards with surprise. 'The factory number! And what did they look like? Where are they now?'

'They left, and walked down the street in this direction. I don't know what they looked like. Only the children were at home,' said Mother.

Uncle Cosmo looked ashen. 'I thought I would be followed. But I didn't know they were so close. If only I knew what they looked like. Alicia, please don't call the police just yet. I would like a little time to try and figure out who is behind this. If I don't work this out first, I fear that many people could be unfairly implicated. Justice can be very rough sometimes in Kenya. It is not necessarily the person holding the gun who is directing the action.'

'Oh dear,' she said, concerned. 'Hopefully we can solve this together. Sleep well, Cosmo. We'll come and see you in the morning.' Mother gave him another hug and left.

As she walked down the garden path, she stepped carefully over trailing brambles, but did not see the two men watching her from the shadows beyond the path.

The Disappearance

Bella had no idea that Uncle Cosmo had arrived in Paradise Road the previous night. She was not the first awake at the Pink House: Lucky was, and Lucky woke Bella as usual by licking her feet. Out of her bedroom window Bella saw the sun was just rising. She was happy when she thought of the chocolate – but then sad when she remembered the ivory. She wondered again how the ivory had come to be inside the chocolate. She still thought that the best thing was to ring Uncle Cosmo in Africa. He had to be back from holiday soon and surely he could help sort out this mess. She had overheard her father talking about it with Uncle Rupert and Aunt Alicia the night before.

Despite the ivory and there being no more chocolate for breakfast, Bella was still pleased to be awake. It was 5.45 a.m. She wondered if it was too early to go and see her cousins. It probably was. She woke Johnny instead to see if he wanted to come with her to take Lucky for a walk.

Meanwhile, at Wisteria House, Freddie, Rose and Tom had been wide awake since 5.30 a.m. They had gone downstairs to make a hearty English breakfast for Uncle Cosmo: fried bacon and eggs, sausages and tomatoes placed between two fresh thick-cut slices of bread, which they wrapped in tinfoil to keep warm.

The children left Wisteria House. They headed off quietly down the road, feeling a little nervous. They did not see anyone: the whole world seemed to be asleep. The sky was streaked with pink; it was a beautiful morning. Just then, as Freddie, Rose and Tom walked towards 52 Paradise Road, they heard the sound of running behind them. Then Lucky bounded past, and when they looked back they saw Bella and Johnny were running to catch up.

'What are you doing out this early?' asked Bella breathlessly.

'Uncle Cosmo,' Freddie replied.

'Uncle Cosmo?' asked Johnny.

'Shh, not here.' Tom looked about anxiously. 'We'll tell you soon.'

'Come,' said Rose, and she led them quickly and quietly down to 52 Paradise Road. The garden was wild. The path down the side of the house was overgrown with brambles that scratched at the children's legs. But they were careful and held branches back for each other, and passed relatively unscathed.

When they reached the back door they were surprised that it was open. The children looked at the overgrown garden, but could not see anyone. They peered into the house, and saw nothing unusual. Nervously they ventured inside.

In the early morning light the sun shone through the window. It seemed to highlight all the little dust particles hanging in the air. Rose gasped.

'What?' whispered Johnny.

'Look,' said Rose quietly, pointing. There on the kitchen table was the lovely meal prepared by her mother for Uncle Cosmo, looking as if it had barely been eaten. The basket beside it also looked untouched.

Johnny still did not understand. 'It's just someone's old dinner. That is nothing to be afraid of.'

'No,' said Tom. 'That is not just someone's old dinner. It is Uncle Cosmo's dinner.'

'Uncle Cosmo!' said Johnny and Bella in surprise.

'Yes,' continued Tom. 'That is what we wanted to tell you. He came here last night and Mother prepared a small supper for him. Uncle Cosmo decided it was better for everyone if he slept here. He was tired and wet and cold. He looked dreadful. But why didn't he eat his dinner?'

'The bad men!' said Rose.

'Bad men?' asked Johnny and Bella.

'Let's not jump to conclusions!' said Tom. 'We had a visit from two policemen. But we think that they may have been imposters, and could have just been wearing stolen uniforms.'

'Maybe Uncle Cosmo's asleep,' suggested Freddie.

'Let's look for Uncle Cosmo,' said Bella. She and Lucky set off upstairs, followed closely by the others, except Rose, who just stood there staring at the dust and the barely touched dinner.

They climbed upstairs, avoiding the second-to-last step, because they all knew it creaked terribly. Bella and Lucky went towards the first bedroom. Bella opened the door slowly. Nothing. Just dust and an old bed. Then the second bedroom: again nothing. Along the corridor was a third bedroom. The door opened – thankfully it didn't creak.

But what a shock! Bella's heart began to beat very loudly. There on a double bed lay the two policemen, snoring. Bella closed the door quietly.

Finally, in the last bedroom, the children found Uncle Cosmo. He was tied up and lying on the floor. He was not moving. Bella rushed to his side and rolled him over. It was very hard to tell if he was dead or just asleep. The children looked at each other. Then Bella quietly started to untie the knots. They all helped. Bella thought if he was just sleeping, they would need to wake him very quietly. Lucky started to point her nose to the door, and nudge Bella. But Bella was a very determined person: once she had begun a task her concentration was intense. She ignored Lucky and focused only on untying the rope.

Johnny, Freddie and Tom were also busy trying to untie the knots. No one heard the door behind them opening. Lucky barked, as one of the thugs, PC Everest, walked into the room.

13

The Writing in the Dust

In the meantime, PC Everest's companion had woken up, stretched, looked out of the window and then gone downstairs to get a glass of water. Imagine his surprise when he found Rose in the kitchen. But Rose was close to the door and she ran. She ran down the side path, through the brambles, not even caring as they scratched her legs. She had never run so fast in her whole life. She did not stop running until she arrived at the door of her own home.

She leaned on the doorbell. Her parents did not

answer the door. She rang again. Still no answer. She knocked. Were they asleep upstairs?

For Rose it felt like an eternity. She looked down the garden path but could not see very much of the road beyond the tall box hedge. She kept ringing the bell. She thought she could hear the sound of running – feet running – getting nearer and nearer.

Father dreamed of hammering, again and again. Mother dreamed of a fire. An alarm was sounding in her dream. Then there was actual ringing. They sat bolt upright. Then they leapt out of bed, grabbing their dressing gowns, and flew downstairs. Who could it be? And at this early hour!

As soon as her father opened the front door, Rose collapsed into his arms. At that same moment, Lucky came rushing around the corner, alone. Lucky looked at Rose's face and then at her bleeding legs and then back again, panting, with a concerned look in her eyes. It was the same look that Rose's parents had on their faces.

Rose's parents were shocked to see her. Blood was running down her legs.

'Oh, Rose!' cried Mother. 'Ma chérie, what has happened to you? Are you okay?'

Then Mother realised with horror there was no sign of Freddie or Tom.

'Help . . . others . . . Fifty-two . . . house . . . policemen there,' was all Rose could splutter between sobs.

It was enough. Her father understood immediately. Without waiting for an explanation he ran, his dressing gown flapping behind him.

At 52 Paradise Road the fake policemen had forced the children down the stairs and out of the house, and carried the unconscious body of Uncle Cosmo with them. They marched the children to the shed, and dragged Uncle Cosmo through the long grass, criss-crossed with sharp brambles that had woven themselves into the overgrown lawn. In the tumbledown garden shed they tied up their hostages. The children were scared to see two other men, both in white underwear, and both unconscious like Uncle Cosmo. Johnny thought that these two men looked as if they would have fitted the police uniforms a lot better than the two men currently wearing them.

Once they had tied the children and Uncle Cosmo securely, the policemen returned to the house.

Meanwhile, Mother took Rose inside and made her a cup of cocoa. Rose clasped the cup: she felt calm, but tears still streamed down her face. Her mother wrapped her arms around her and gave her a long hug. After that Rose told her mother the full story. It was quite short. Mother gasped when she heard about the untouched basket and dinner, and of how Rose had run to escape when one of the visitors from the night before had entered the kitchen.

Uncle Cosmo's pursuers watched Father through the upper-floor window as he approached the house. They quickly fastened the last buttons on their uniforms and slipped into their roles as bobbies on the beat. It was important to them that the children's parents did not search 52 Paradise Road or interrupt their search for the chocolate.

PC Everest and PC Strong left the house and tried to walk Father back down the front path, but he refused to leave.

'Hello, sir, is this your home?' asked PC Everest.

'No,' said Father. 'No, it is not mine.'

'Then what you are doing here?' asked PC Strong.

'Looking for my children, and my brother. Do you mind if I step past?'

'No need, sir; the house is empty. Neighbours reported a disturbance. We've just looked and there is no one there,' announced PC Everest.

'Still, I would like to see for myself,' said Father.

'Of course,' said PC Everest, confidently letting him pass. He knew he would find nothing in the house.

'Mind if we join you?' asked PC Everest.

'No, please do,' replied Father.

'If they're with your brother, then why are you worried?' asked PC Strong in a slightly sarcastic tone.

'No, they are not with my brother. My daughter came here this morning to visit him, and was with her brothers, I believe. Rose arrived home scared, bleeding and without her siblings! So I came immediately to find them.'

The policemen progressed through the house

with Father. They found no evidence of any children. They walked back down the garden path, leading Father out of the house and away from the garden.

As they stood on the footpath outside the house PC Everest asked a trick question: 'Have you checked for them at home, sir?'

'No. I have not,' responded Father.

'Then we suggest you start there, sir,' said PC Strong, in the kindest and most hopeful tone he could muster.

Father's mouth dropped. He was momentarily lost for words. 'But . . . what makes you think that they might be there?'

'Well,' said PC Everest, 'had you considered that the others may not have joined your daughter at this hour? It is very early. They might just be asleep.'

'No,' said Father. 'I guess I had assumed that they'd all come together.'

'We suggest you check there first,' said PC Strong. 'But let me assure you we will take this very seriously.'

'Yes, leave it with us,' added PC Everest, cunningly buying a little more time. 'We will file a missing persons report immediately and be in touch shortly. Where do you live?'

'Seventeen Paradise Road. Just down there,' said Father, vaguely pointing down the road. PC Everest pulled a real police notebook out of his uniform pocket, and wrote down the address.

'And the names of the missing children?' asked PC Everest, carefully noting down the answer. Father spelled out their names, and felt relieved that the police were taking it seriously.

'And finally your mobile number to get in touch as soon as possible,' asked PC Everest, carefully noting it down.

The police turned and walked to the end of the street to the crossroads. Father heard one of them grumbling to the other, in a stage whisper, as they turned right in the direction of the little lane: 'Looked as if he'd lost his marbles. Did you see the slippers and that ancient dressing gown?'

'Yes, I imagine one does feel half crazy if one loses one's children. We must do all we can to help him.'

Father felt reassured by the last comment. But

the dust told another tale. If Father had paused a moment longer, he might have seen the answer on the windowpane in the fourth bedroom, written in the dust.

The Search

Father walked home. Perhaps the police were right, and he would find his children in bed. The once-grand house had certainly seemed empty. He felt disappointed. Uncle Cosmo had vanished before he had even seen him.

If only Father had stayed a little longer, and had been just a little more observant, he too might have noticed the little details like the fit of the policemen's uniforms. He might also have heard the gate at the far end of the garden creak on its rusted hinges as it was pushed open from the other side. He would also have seen the very same policemen, PC Everest and PC Strong, return to their captives, whom they had hidden most carefully in the garden shed, together with the inert body of Uncle Cosmo. If only he had thought to check the shed he would also have seen two bound-up and real policemen who were wearing nothing more than white vests and underpants!

It was still not clear to the children whether Uncle Cosmo was alive or dead. All they knew was that he had not moved or spoken and had not even opened his eyes during the whole ordeal. But Freddie thought he had seen Uncle Cosmo breathing.

When the policemen returned, they spat out their demands. They wanted to know where the chocolate was.

'Chocolate? What chocolate?' said Tom, as innocently as he could. But the policemen were no more satisfied with this answer than they had been the last time.

Mother cried when Father returned without her children. Rose had told her that they had been at the house looking for Uncle Cosmo. Father said they had to go to Uncle Crispin's house to ask him to help look for their lost children. They left Rose at home, safe and warm, having a cup of hot chocolate in the kitchen. Lucky was sitting at her feet and Socrates purring on her lap. Her parents knocked on Uncle Crispin's door. He was still asleep, but soon roused himself and came downstairs rubbing his eyes.

When Father and Mother told Uncle Crispin that Freddie and Tom were missing, his face fell. Father said that Lucky was with Rose keeping her company. They asked Uncle Crispin to help them look for the children. He suggested he wake Aunt Lily, Johnny and Bella and then everyone could help search for them.

Uncle Crispin returned a few moments later. He said, 'Johnny and Bella are gone too. They must be with Freddie and Tom. That would explain why Lucky was out so early.'

Aunt Lily appeared, looking ashen. 'We must call the police!' she cried.

'I have already spoken to the police and they will file a missing persons report,' said Father.

'Have you tried calling the children yet?' asked Aunt Lily.

'Yes, and texted them, but there has been no answer,' said Father.

'Then where shall we look?' asked Aunt Lily.

Uncle Crispin suggested, 'Let's go back to Fifty-two Paradise Road and check there.'

'But the police have already checked Fifty-two Paradise Road, and so has Rupert,' said Mother. 'So that would just be a waste of time.'

'They can't have got far,' said Father.

'Perhaps we should check the train station and nearby streets?' said Aunt Lily.

'We could go by bike to be faster and cover the parks and the Thames riverside too,' suggested Uncle Crispin. They all agreed. Aunt Lily and Uncle Crispin quickly put on jackets over their pyjamas. Not a moment was lost as they went off in search of their children. But Father and Mother had completely forgotten about Rose, believing that she was safe at home with Lucky and Socrates.

15

The Captives

Back at the abandoned house, the captors were torturing their captives. They started with water, spraying them with water pistols, and demanding answers.

'Chocolate!' PC Everest growled at the children. 'Where is it?'

'Who knows?' said Johnny. He was sprayed in the face.

'You there, the girl, you're lying. Where's the chocolate?'

'I d-d-d-don't know,' stuttered Bella nervously.

'She's lying!' yelled PC Everest.

'And you, boy – yes, you,' he said, spraying Freddie full in the face. 'Your face tells me you are lying. Where is it?'

'I don't know,' spluttered Freddie truthfully. He didn't know where his uncle had hidden the chocolate.

The fat policeman spoke to the skinny one, with a half-smile twisting his lip: 'I heard that the best way to get the truth out of little blighters like these is to take their hands and tie them to their feet. Then you sprinkle them with sugar and have a goat lick it off. They spit the truth out every time.'

'Well, that sounds like a fine suggestion!' said PC Everest sarcastically. 'Shall we pop down to the shops for a packet of sugar and an old goat?'

Bella tried to stifle a giggle at the thought of these odd policemen trying to buy an old goat in this city.

'You nasty little girl. Why are you laughing?' said PC Strong. The fat policeman was so annoyed that he kicked the old box that she was sitting on. It gave her a fright and she nearly fell off.

'You're just a daft idiot! Where are you going to get a live goat around here?' the skinny policeman taunted the fat one, throwing a cup of water over him and falling over laughing at his own joke.

PC Strong walked over and swiftly thumped PC Everest's skinny arm. Then they both started punching each other, very hard.

'ENOUGH!' shouted the fat policeman. 'We need to focus on finding the chocolate and getting out of here.' They pulled back, stopped punching and glared at each other.

'Where do you live?' PC Everest asked menacingly. His face was within an inch of Johnny's face. His breath smelled of stale peppermints.

'You've been to our house,' interjected Tom quickly. 'You know it's in this street, Number Seventeen.'

'I was not talking to you,' he snarled at Tom. He turned back to Johnny. 'Big boy, where do you live?'

'Number One,' Johnny said softly.

'Speak up boy. Number One what?' asked PC Strong, who was standing so close that Johnny could smell his unpleasant stale body odour.

'Number One Paradise Road,' Johnny answered.

'Where's that?' asked PC Strong.

'This *is* Paradise Road,' said PC Everest, and added, 'You dumbo.'

'I'm not so dumb. I reckon the chocolate is there. We just have to search their houses. These cunning little kids have hidden it from us,' retorted PC Strong.

'Hmmph,' said PC Everest, giving PC Strong a pitying look. 'You know, George, it's quite hard to hide a tea chest full of chocolate!'

The policemen left together for Number 1 Paradise Road. They just missed seeing the children's parents leaving on their bicycles.

'Oh gawd,' said PC Strong as they approached the Pink House. 'Would you look at the colour of that house!'

'It sure is pink,' said his tall companion. 'It looks as if it would be at home on top of a wedding cake,' he joked.

PC Strong did not laugh, he grunted. He kept watch from the doorstep of the Pink House, while PC Everest bent forward and began to break the lock.

16

The Stranger

As soon as Rose had finished her hot chocolate, Lucky starting pulling at the bottom of her skirt. Rose knew what Lucky wanted: she wanted to go back to the abandoned house to look for the others.

'We'll go, Lucky, I promise. But let's wait until Mother and Father get back.' Lucky then walked to the door and pawed at it.

Rose glanced out of the window and jumped. There was a strange lady coming up the path: sublimely dressed, wearing a camel-coloured suit, with a very delicate collar trimmed in matching fur. Her shoes were high, in a soft peachy-orange colour that complemented her silk scarf, light summer gloves and pretty auburn hair. She wore big dark glasses, and carried a small, tan, crocodile-skin suitcase and handbag. She knocked and Rose opened the door.

'Hello,' said Rose hesitantly. Lucky was about to run down the path, but thought better of it, and stayed protectively by Rose's side, growling softly.

'Hello.' The lady smiled. 'I'm looking for Cosmo Baker's brother Rupert. Do you know if I have the right address?'

'Yes, you have,' replied Rose.

'Ah, you have such pretty red hair! I am guessing you must be Rose.'

'Yes,' said Rose, staring at her and wondering how this stranger knew her name.

'I am Josephine, Cosmo's girlfriend. I came as soon as I heard.'

'I didn't know he had a girlfriend,' said Rose cautiously.

Josephine smiled. 'I think he has.'

Maybe it was the warm way Josephine smiled, or the silence that now hung between them, but Rose found herself asking Josephine, 'Would you like to come in?'

As soon as she had asked, and Josephine had stepped inside, Rose worried whether it had been the right thing to do. But then Rose reasoned that her parents would have invited Cosmo's girlfriend inside if they had been there. It would be rude to keep her standing on the doorstep. And besides, her parents would be home soon, thought Rose.

'When Cosmo's secretary told me he'd left, I just had to come and find him. I've been so worried about him,' said Josephine.

Josephine put down her small suitcase and then removed her jacket to reveal a cream silk blouse. Rose offered her a cup of tea.

'Oh, I would just love a cup,' said Josephine as she took off her glasses. 'A day does not seem complete without one, and I haven't had a cup yet. It has been a long journey.' Josephine smiled at Rose and looked a little tired. Rose felt almost instantly that she could trust Josephine.

Rose made a cup of tea. When Josephine asked if Rose had seen Cosmo, Rose told her everything that had happened so far. Josephine said, 'I am shocked. Ivory in the chocolate! How on earth could it have got in there?' Then Josephine said, almost as if she were speaking to herself, 'So that is why he left suddenly.' She seemed relieved and then concerned. She looked at Rose intensely. 'I know Cosmo well: he would never do such a thing!'

As Josephine stirred the sugar into her third cup of tea, Rose noticed her bangle. It was mostly black, with small inlaid flecks of white. A beautiful shape. All soft curves, with a sparkling diamond.

'What a lovely bracelet, Josephine!' she heard herself saying, to distract her momentarily from her worries. She liked Josephine, and for the second time since meeting her she surprised herself; she did not often notice jewellery. But this piece seemed special.

'Oh, thank you,' said Josephine. 'It is very old. It was given to me by my grandmother. If you look carefully you will see that it is a beautiful bird. See its glittery little eye: that is a diamond. It is made from ebony, which is a very hard wood: the same wood that is used to make the black keys on a piano. And the small flecks of white are ivory, which they used to use to make the white keys. Of course today they don't make the white keys from ivory, thank goodness. And if you look carefully, you can see its beak and legs wrap around my wrist. I always loved it as a child, so my grandmother said that one day it would be mine.'

'It is beautifully carved, but I didn't see the bird until you showed me,' replied Rose.

'Yes, until you know, you just see the lovely undulating curves. I love it. It always reminds me of my grandmother. She was so kind and loving. I miss her. I wear it every day.'

For a moment, she seemed wistful, and then she smiled and changed the subject. 'Shall I tell you a big secret?' Her eyes sparkled and at that moment she looked truly happy.

17

The Secret

'Cosmo and I are engaged to be married,' said Josephine. 'It's a secret at the moment, okay, so don't tell anyone.'

Rose was thrilled. Even though she had only just met Josephine she liked her very much already.

And then Rose found herself asking, 'Have you enough bridesmaids?'

Josephine laughed. 'I see. Well, I have two, and I have a sister, but I do need another one. Are you very good at carrying a large bunch of flowers?'

'Yes,' said Rose seriously. 'I think I could be.'

'Then you have got the job,' Josephine beamed.

'But now tell me more about Cosmo. How was he when you saw him?'

Rose was honest. 'Josephine, I don't know. When he arrived at the garden door he looked exhausted. I barely recognised him. Then this morning at the house I didn't see him. I don't even know if he was still there. Would you like to go to look for yourself?'

'From what you have told me I still think there is a possibility that the rotten crooks will return to Number Fifty-two. After all, they must want the ivory. Perhaps they have taken the children as hostages to lead them to the chocolate? That might explain why they have not returned yet. Would you be too frightened to return?'

'No, not me,' said Rose bravely. 'I'm worried about the others. I want to go. I don't need to wait for Mother and Father. I'm desperate to find them.'

'Let's go!' said Josephine. As she opened the door, Lucky dashed out and ran ahead.

'Lucky!' Rose called. Lucky ran back and they all walked together towards the abandoned house.

The Abandoned House

Josephine, Rose and Lucky arrived at 52 Paradise Road. It was eerily quiet. Their footsteps echoed around the empty house as they went further inside.

Rose stared at the forlorn and half-eaten shepherd's pie that was still in the kitchen. She walked around the ground floor while Josephine looked upstairs.

Josephine seemed to glide quietly through the rooms. But she too found nothing.

Lucky had not stopped darting from room to room. She seemed to be following the scent of Johnny, Bella, Freddie, and Tom. But Lucky was so fast that Rose gave up keeping pace with her.

Rose paused for some time at the window. She thought she saw something in the garden. It was terribly overgrown. Great brambles laced across the old lawn. Once-orderly English borders were now shaggy and out of control. Only the old apple tree still looked pretty, with its young summer fruit ripening slowly in the midsummer sun. Rose saw a blackbird in the apple tree. It flitted to the roof of a tumbledown garden shed. Rose paused. What had she seen? A flicker of movement out of the corner of her eye? It must have been the birds in the tree, she thought. She moved to the next room.

Step by step, they progressed through the empty rooms: Josephine silent and observant, Rose nervous but determined. They reached the fourth bedroom: there was an unmade bed, the curtains were drawn, and just enough light seeped inside to suggest it had been occupied not too long ago. Josephine walked across the room to draw the curtains back. As she looked out she noticed the writing in the dirt of the windowpane: 'Beware the Blackbird'.

Lucky barked from somewhere in the house.

'What's that?' asked Rose.

'What?' said Josephine.

'Over there,' said Rose, pointing to a white piece of paper on the floor near Josephine's feet.

Josephine stooped down to pick it up quickly. 'Just a blank piece of paper.' She began to crumple it in her hand.

'Oh, no, it isn't,' murmured Rose as she took the paper and held it in the light. She squinted at the blank page. 'Johnny might have used his invisible pen. Perhaps it's a clue!'

Rose fumbled in her pocket, and out came a pen with a little fluorescent light at the end.

'We all have these pens ever since Bella's last birthday.' Rose shone the light on the paper. It said: 'Help. Ivory hunters! Cosmo might be dead.'

Josephine let out a little cry.

Lucky barked again. She sounded further away,

and more urgent. Rose and Josephine ran downstairs.

'Lucky! Where are you?' cried Rose. 'She must have found the others.' Then Rose remembered that she had thought she had seen something in the garden. 'I think the barking is coming from the garden,' she called to Josephine.

Once outside, they moved cautiously. The brambles were entwined with everything and seemed determined to keep them from crossing the lawn. Then Lucky barked again.

'I think Lucky is in the little shed over there near the end of the garden,' said Rose. Even though she was dressed in clothes not suited to running, Josephine seemed to fly through the thorns to the shed.

Is Uncle Cosmo Dead?

There was a bolt on the outside of the weathered wooden door of the shed. Josephine slid it back and opened the door. She immediately saw the body of a man.

'Cosmo!' cried Josephine.

In two steps she was by his side. She gently took his battered body and cradled him in her arms. 'Who has done this to you, my darling?' Cosmo was still.

Josephine kissed him gently. Silent tears rolled

down her cheeks. Four children were watching her suspiciously.

'Who are you?' asked Freddie, staring at her.

'I'm Cosmo's girlfriend,' said Josephine.

'Why are you here?' asked Bella.

'I followed Cosmo,' Josephine answered simply.

Lucky was trying to untie the rope with her teeth, but was not succeeding. Rose arrived. Johnny, Bella, Freddie and Tom quickly filled her in on what she'd missed.

'They got us so fast!' said Freddie.

'The skinny policeman, PC Everest, pointed a gun at us and made us hand over our mobile phones. The gun looked real. I am still not sure if it was real. We were scared,' said Bella.

'We barely had time to do anything,' added Tom. 'He briefly put his head out of the door to call for the fat one – you know, PC Strong. I had time to scribble you a note. I dropped it beside Uncle Cosmo's bed. Did you find it?'

'Yes, thank you,' said Rose. 'I knew it was a clue.'

'I found another clue too,' added Josephine. 'In

the rush I forgot to tell you that there was a message in the dust, "Beware the Blackbird", but I didn't know what it meant.'

'Uncle Cosmo might know,' said Bella. 'If you found the note in that room, it was his room.'

Johnny added, 'We should follow the policemen. We know where they went. One is fat and stupid, but he is strong.'

Bella said, 'The skinny one is mean.'

Freddie observed wisely, 'And greedy . . . for the ivory.'

Bella agreed, 'Yes. Yet neither seems to have much of a plan. There must be someone else.'

Tom added, 'And now they are at Uncle Crispin's house trying to find our chocolate!'

'Where is this chocolate?' asked Josephine. 'Why not just give it to them and have them gone? The beasts.'

'Because it's wrong to kill elephants and sell their tusks, and they should go to prison,' said Johnny.

'But first we must help Cosmo. He needs a doctor,' said Josephine.

Rose agreed. 'Yes, let them have the chocolate! We need to get Uncle Cosmo to hospital. And who are these other two?' she asked, pointing at the two men in their underwear, also in the shed, but seemingly knocked out.

'We think that these two might be real policemen, and that the other two stole their uniforms,' said Bella.

Tom took charge. 'Let's get our priorities right. First, we need a doctor. Then second, ring the police and let them catch these crooks.'

But just as he said this Uncle Cosmo stirred. Josephine stroked his head. His eyelids fluttered a little, and one eye opened, and then the other.

'Josephine,' he murmured, 'what are you doing here?' and smiled.

'I came as soon as your secretary told me you had to flee. I was worried about you. Are you feeling okay?' asked Josephine.

'It's so good to see you. But my head hurts. Did I fall?' asked Uncle Cosmo.

'No,' said Bella kindly. 'Those mean men must

have hit you. When we found you, you were unconscious and tied up.'

'Bella!' he exclaimed, 'Tom!' Uncle Cosmo seemed to focus slowly, 'Rose! Freddie! And Johnny! How wonderful to see you. Ah yes, now I remember. I was in the bedroom upstairs, on the phone to my secretary; she was saying something about a blackbird. I couldn't make sense of it. And then I don't remember anything.'

'You need a doctor!' said Josephine.

'I feel fine. Just a bit stiff,' replied Uncle Cosmo. He looked around the shed. 'And who are these two fine gentlemen lying here in their underwear?' he asked.

'We think that these two are the real PC Strong and PC Everest,' said Johnny.

'What about those men who were following me? Do we know where they are?' asked Uncle Cosmo.

'Yes, the men went to our house to look for the chocolate, but we don't know where it is. Father hid it somewhere when we realised how dangerous the ivory was,' answered Bella.

'What are we waiting for? Let's catch these crooked men,' said Uncle Cosmo, pulling himself slowly and painfully to his feet.

The Chase

As they hurried down the road, Josephine said: 'Someone has to ring the police too. This is getting out of hand. And Cosmo, you need a doctor.'

Uncle Cosmo agreed. 'Good idea, Josephine. Why don't you ring the police? Tell them it's urgent! We haven't a moment to spare. I want to catch the little rotters who have infiltrated my factory. I need to know who it is and stop them from causing more harm.'

With Uncle Cosmo leading them back to the Pink

House at the start of the road, the children felt brave and fearless.

'Okay,' said Josephine. 'I left my handbag and phone at your house, Rose.' As they all passed 17 Paradise Road, Rose took Josephine inside Wisteria House to find the small crocodile handbag.

At Wisteria House Josephine rang the police. She reported an armed break-in at 1 Paradise Road. Just as she hung up Josephine remembered something: she paused and redialled. 'Ambulance. There are two men, unconscious and tied up, in the garden shed at Fifty-two Paradise Road . . . No, I do not know what happened to them. But they are in urgent need of medical attention,' said Josephine, and hung up swiftly. 'Let's go!' she said.

Meanwhile, Johnny and Bella led Uncle Cosmo, Freddie and Tom into their house. As they entered, it was so quiet that they thought there was no one there. The house was a mess. They walked around the ground floor looking for the crooked policemen. No one. They went upstairs. Nothing. They walked into the first bedroom: it was empty. But the door on the other side of the room was closed. So they tiptoed across the bedroom towards it. They were halfway across the room when the door behind them slammed.

It was the skinny policeman. Everyone froze. 'Were you missing us?' he asked. Then he grabbed Bella by her thick black hair and pointed his gun at her temple.

'Tie them up, George.' George pulled Bella's arms roughly behind her and cuffed them tightly with rope. It hurt.

Uncle Cosmo looked at the policemen. 'George and Patrick. What are you doing here? You should be at work in the factory!'

'You're not the boss here,' Patrick snarled, standing as tall as he could. He glared at Uncle Cosmo.

George asked aggressively, 'Whose house is this?' He was pointing his gun at Uncle Cosmo.

'Ours,' said Bella and Johnny together.

'You told us you had no tea chest,' sneered Patrick. 'But guess what we've found in the garden. Empty!

WHERE did you hide the chocolate, you nasty little blighters?'

The two men then moved from one room to the next, tipping up furniture and tearing out drawers. They looked under beds, behind doors, *almost* everywhere.

'It must be here somewhere. You little skunk!' Patrick said, this time pulling Tom upwards by his hair.

'He doesn't even live here,' said Bella.

'Pick on someone your own size,' growled Uncle Cosmo. 'Pull *my* hair, you dirty rat.' In different circumstances this might have been funny, as Uncle Cosmo had barely a hair on his shiny head. But no one laughed.

'So where is it?' yelled Patrick, who had moved very close to Uncle Cosmo's face while losing his temper. He was angry at being called a dirty rat.

Its pink colour was not the only odd thing about 1 Paradise Road. It had originally been built with many half-levels. These quirky features had mostly been removed during some renovation work. But there remained an under-floor cupboard, accessed through a type of trapdoor. Fortunately, burglars are lazy creatures: it's how they ended up in the game they are in. They rarely think of looking up, or down, for that matter; they are generally in a hurry and look in only the most obvious places.

The two ruffians continued to march the children and Uncle Cosmo through the house, goading them, sometimes threatening them, but they were no nearer to discovering the location of the chocolate. When they got to the office, where the secret under-floor cupboard was, the children stood very still. They did not know where Uncle Crispin had hidden the chocolate. But the trapdoor hid a half-height room, surely big enough to hide the large blocks of chocolate.

The Hidden Chocolate

Josephine and Rose hurried to the Pink House at 1 Paradise Road to join the others. When they arrived there was no one to be seen. The front door was shut and they did not have a key. Rose was about to ring the bell, when Josephine stopped her.

'Is there another way in? We don't want to alert those crooks that we are here,' Josephine said. 'The element of surprise is always an advantage'.

'There's a spare key hidden in the garden.' Rose led Josephine down the driveway. Josephine was tall enough to reach her hand over the gate and pull the bolt. On entering the garden, they looked up at the house. At first nothing seemed out of place. But then they saw some shapes through a third-floor window, in Uncle Crispin's office. Josephine looked pale and scared. They were holding guns.

'They want the ivory – they do not want to kill anyone,' Rose tried to reassure her. She hoped she was right. Determined, she went into the shed quickly, and found the key. Then Rose, Josephine and Lucky quietly slipped in through the back door.

'Wait. Let's open the front door,' whispered Josephine. 'Then the police can come straight in.'

While they were opening the door as quietly as possible, Lucky shot upstairs. Johnny, Bella, Freddie and Tom were in the office, trying really hard not to look at the floor. Under the desk were the two flat brass handles of the trapdoor. Bella was convinced that the chocolate must be there.

George and Patrick were pulling out drawers, opening cupboards, roughly emptying the contents, and threatening their captives with pinches and pokes. There was a slight noise on the stairs and Lucky burst in, growling. She sprang up on Patrick, causing him to fall backward and drop his gun.

Everyone looked down at the gun, which fell near the brass handles. Quick as a flash, Bella placed her foot on the handle and the other on the gun, so neither George nor Patrick could easily retrieve it. As her hands were tied she could not pick it up.

Bella's attempt to hide the cupboard had been just a fraction too late. Both intruders dived towards the handles, and together pulled them up. There lay the dark brown chocolate. They grabbed it. Patrick kissed it and George laughed triumphantly.

As they embraced the chocolate, neither noticed Josephine and Rose appear. But what stopped the nasty men in their tracks gave everyone a surprise. It wasn't Rose picking up the gun, her hands trembling as she pointed it at them. It was the stern voice of Josephine.

'Patrick Alexander Plumb! George Wharton Grimble! What are you doing?' They looked up at her guiltily. 'You were such good boys. What about your mother, Patrick? Mrs Plumb was such a fine woman. George, what would dear old Ma Grimble say? Didn't she always tell you to keep your nose clean and work hard? Stand up straight. You ought to be ashamed of yourselves.' She paused and thought for a moment. 'Whose idea was this? Who put you up to this?'

Both men stood up. They blushed. Bella thought that they looked like children caught stealing.

'His – GG's,' said Patrick, nodding towards George.

'No, it was Patrick's idea,' said George.

'What would you want to do with all that ivory and chocolate?' Josephine asked, looking at the contents of the hidden cupboard.

'We could not help it. See, it was the Blackbird who made us do it,' mumbled George.

'The blackbird?' asked Josephine.

'Yes, *you know*, the Blackbird! You know. You do know,' he said, meaningfully looking her straight in the eye.

Just then, two further police constables arrived.

These ones looked real, and seemed to know whom they were after. Immediately they arrested George Grimble and Patrick Plumb. Then they individually questioned everyone else. To Uncle Cosmo's surprise and dismay, they then arrested Josephine too. Cosmo could not believe it. Tears filled his eyes.

'Not Josephine. No, not my Josephine,' he whispered. 'She wouldn't do such a thing!' You could hear the pain in his voice at the very thought of her being involved in this crime.

One of the constables explained: 'To arrest someone, sir, we need reasonable grounds to suspect they are involved in a crime. Having questioned everyone here, it is our reasonable belief that this woman is the Blackbird. She is the ultimate mastermind behind it all.'

'But she called you!' said Rose to the policemen. 'I saw her.' Rose tried to stare as hard as she could at one of the police, challenging him. He was unmoved.

'Sounds like a clever double-bluff to me,' responded the policeman. 'This is a very cunning woman. You need to be clever to trade successfully in ivory and very clever indeed to trade in this quantity.'

'And what about me? Why don't you arrest me too?' asked Uncle Cosmo. 'After all, I sent the package to the children!' There was disbelief in his voice.

'Yes,' said the policeman patiently, 'we did think of arresting you. But since you are handcuffed and have been beaten, we do not think it is reasonable to suspect that you led this crime'.

The other children were not surprised that the police had arrested Josephine. But Rose felt very upset. She was sure that they were wrong, even though she had known Josephine for such a short time. She refused to believe her capable of having one elephant killed, let alone a herd.

The children's parents were worried to find the door to the Pink House wide open, but were then quickly overcome with relief to find all of the children and Lucky safe and well. They hugged everyone, including Uncle Cosmo.

Uncle Crispin checked that the police had found all of the large heavy chocolate bars. He had hidden the half-eaten one separately behind the old fridge in the garage.

Rose could not help but take one last longing look at the enormous quantity of chocolate. She asked the police, 'Can we keep the chocolate and just give you the ivory?'

The policeman smiled and explained: 'At this stage, the chocolate and ivory are all part of the evidence. Perhaps after the trial you might be able to request the return of some of the chocolate.'

George Grimble and Patrick Plumb were led to one police car, while Josephine was led to another. As they helped her into the back seat, Josephine looked up at Uncle Cosmo.

'It's not true,' Josephine said. 'I am not the Blackbird.'

Uncle Cosmo said, 'Of course you wouldn't be. Impossible.' He glared at the constable and then sighed as the police car door was shut.

Rose was standing beside Uncle Cosmo. He put his arm around her and said, as much to himself as to Rose, 'I'm sure that the police will just ask her a few questions and then she'll be free to go. They can't believe she helped those villains. I am sure she is not involved. It's just ridiculous to think she had any control over them. The fact that she wears a blackbird bracelet is a coincidence!'

Rose felt terrible when she heard this. She realised that she had included Josephine's bracelet in her account to the police. She hoped that she had not got Josephine further into trouble. But the other children remembered Josephine's voice, and the crooks' reaction to it. They thought the woman who had stopped the crooks with her voice alone was obviously in charge of the whole operation.

And was this not a suitable end? The false policemen imprisoned behind bars, and the woman in control of them soon to be locked safely away. The Blackbird had been caught. The children could all sleep soundly that night. All except Rose.

Who is the Blackbird?

Over the next days, Uncle Cosmo looked pale and withdrawn. He showered and tidied himself up. He ate some proper home-cooked food. He had even been to the doctor. But he had never felt, nor looked, more wretched.

The children rallied around, trying to distract him. They thought up useful projects he could help with. He climbed the highest tree in the garden for them and fixed a strong new rope. It was knotted with a special bowline on the bite and a couple of half hitches. He felt confident it would hold. Attached to the other end was an old tractor tyre. It made for a great swing. Three of them could sit comfortably, and five at a pinch. They could get such momentum that it made Bella's stomach flip and Rose squeal with delight. It was even better than the old swing he had made several years ago. Bigger and stronger. The old swing now looked as if it was for little children, thought Bella.

Even though Uncle Cosmo was helpful and involved, he often looked sad. Rose knew that he was thinking of Josephine. He seemed utterly heartbroken. Uncle Cosmo could not even contemplate that she could be capable of such cruelty to elephants. He knew that a family of elephants had died just for the ivory in that one tea chest alone.

Uncle Cosmo thought of the gracious ebony elephants marching across his grandmother's mantelpiece: each one different and carved from a real-life model. They were such majestic creatures. On his adventures, a family of elephants was one of his favourite things to see.

Rose overheard her parents and Uncle Cosmo speaking about it. She heard her father Rupert saying, 'Cosmo, people change. How well do you really know Josephine? Perhaps she changed and you didn't realise.'

'Now, where have I heard that before?' interrupted Mother, looking rather critically at Father as she brought them both a cup of tea.

Rose called a meeting at the end of the garden. Johnny, Bella, Tom, Freddie and Lucky perched on a little stone circle they had collected especially for their deliberations.

'It's not right,' Rose began. 'Josephine can't have been up to no good with those two awful policemen. I just know she is not capable of killing, or having elephants killed. So, what do we actually know? I heard the shock in her voice when she caught those ruffians with the ivory.'

Tom took a stick and on the ground he wrote, 'Beware the Blackbird'. Then he drew a circle and inside wrote an 'S' for secretary.

Bella took up his cue. 'We know that there were

several warnings about someone called the Blackbird. Father said he had been warned by Uncle Cosmo's secretary.' Tom drew a line between the warning and the secretary.

Rose drew another a line between the 'S' for secretary and the warning. She added, 'Then there was a message on the windowpane written in the dust. It also warned of the Blackbird.'

'Even though that was written by Uncle Cosmo, and we know that he was talking to his secretary at the time,' Johnny said as he joined the two lines between the 'S' and the warning. 'This is just the secretary repeating her evidence.'

'We know that Josephine voluntarily told me about her grandmother's bracelet. I would never have even known it was a bird if she hadn't told me,' said Rose. She drew a separate circle with a 'J' in it, for Josephine, but she did not connect it to the warning.

'That story by itself does not connect Josephine with the warning,' said Rose.

'All we know is that Josephine could stop those

two in their tracks by calling them by their full names,' observed Tom.

'But that could be because she's known them since they were small and she obviously knew their families,' added Bella.

'I don't think that anything I saw or heard connects her to the warning about the Blackbird,' said Johnny. 'And didn't she voluntarily tell us about the Blackbird clue written in the dust? Would she really have done that if she was the Blackbird?'

Tom reflected on this. 'Maybe not. Those crooks also suggested Josephine knew the Blackbird. If that's right, then she can't actually be the Blackbird. But do we know of anything, other than a bracelet, that points to Josephine?'

'No,' said Freddie.

Bella said, 'Why don't we go and ask Uncle Cosmo about the warning he received, and about his secretary. I think that we need to know if there's anyone else who has a connection with the factory and a blackbird. If anyone knows, then he does.'

'Good idea, Bella,' said Freddie.

'I'm in,' said Tom. 'I was never quite convinced it was Josephine. She seems too nice.' He smiled at Rose.

'She is kind and thoughtful. I could just tell. Did you know that after she rang the police she also thought to ring for an ambulance. Those two men in the shed might have died if she hadn't done that,' said Rose.

'Aunt Alicia told me that it probably saved their lives,' added Bella.

'George Grimble and Patrick Plumb deserve to go to prison. It was so wicked to beat those two policemen. And tie them up. And all just for their uniforms. I hope they are thrown into prison for a long time,' said Tom.

'I think that Rose is right about Josephine. She was arrested, but they had no real evidence. Let's find out more,' added Johnny.

'Let's try to help her!' said Freddie.

They found Uncle Cosmo sitting at the writing desk. His diary was open, with his pen resting on the page. He was gazing out of the window.

'Uncle Cosmo,' said Johnny directly, 'do you know of any other connection between your factory and a blackbird?'

'That's a good question,' said Uncle Cosmo seriously, as he turned to look at the children. 'I have been thinking of little else. I know every single worker, but none by the name of Blackbird.'

'Think hard, Uncle Cosmo,' urged Rose. 'It doesn't have to be a person. There could be some other connection with a blackbird.'

'Perhaps someone kept one as a pet?' suggested Bella.

'No, not that I recall,' said Uncle Cosmo. 'But you have just given me an idea. My secretary, Doris, does have a very wealthy uncle. He travels in style, with no expense spared. He happily spends money on himself without a thought for the poor in Africa. I don't like him. He is much too selfish. Now, several years ago, maybe even five years ago, people whispered that he owned a spy plane – called a Blackbird. But I never saw it. I thought it was just a rumour. There were only ever a handful of Blackbird spy planes built, and a number of those were supposed to have been lost in accidents. They were never available commercially, but were a stealth plane used by the military. It would be an impossible plane to own. You know, it doesn't even have a door. You'd need to employ a mechanic to bolt you inside. No, I find that very unlikely. But her uncle was a very remote figure, and no one would ever have been close enough to him to find out.' He gazed out of the window, and appeared to be concentrating intently on something in the sky.

'Even his niece?' asked Tom quietly.

But Uncle Cosmo seemed lost in thought and did not appear to have heard Tom. When Uncle Cosmo turned his attention back to the children he said only, 'I need to think. Perhaps I'll call Doris.' He then ambled down the garden to lie in the tyre swing and think about it.

The Arrest

Johnny, Bella, Freddie, Rose and Tom were just talking about what a big mistake it would be to call Doris, if indeed her uncle was the Blackbird, when the doorbell rang. Father and Mother both went to answer the door. It was Johnny and Bella's parents, Uncle Crispin and Aunt Lily. They had been down at the allotment all morning and were carrying a leafy bunch of spinach and some fresh eggs. They wanted to spend some more time with Uncle Cosmo.

'Have you made plans for lunch?' Aunt Lily asked Mother.

'Not until I saw that huge bunch of spinach and thought of bacon, egg and spinach pie!' she laughed.

Aunt Lily said, 'I suggested the same thing to Crispin. But he wanted to see his brothers. Shall we make the pie together?'

'Yes, let's,' smiled Mother as they walked to the kitchen. 'But first a cup of tea or coffee?'

They had just settled down with a cup of coffee when the doorbell rang again.

'This is busier than Piccadilly Circus!' joked Father as he went to answer the door.

Outside were two police officers.

'Hello, can I help?' asked Father.

'Yes, we are looking for a Mr Cosmo Baker. Do you know where we can find him?'

'Certainly. Please come in,' said Father.

Uncle Cosmo was still at the end of the garden, lying in the huge tyre swing and thinking with his eyes closed. He appeared to be half asleep in the early-morning summer sun, and perhaps he was.

'Cosmo, time to wake up. You have to stop sunbathing,' said Father.

'Mmm.'

Father gave him a little shake. 'Come on, Sleeping Beauty. You have some visitors.'

Uncle Cosmo blinked. 'Friends? Josephine!' He leaped up in a rush.

'No, not Josephine!' warned Father. But Uncle Cosmo was already running for the front door.

By the time he reached the front hall, he was slightly out of breath, and surprised to see a policeman and policewoman.

'How is Josephine? Where is Josephine?' asked Uncle Cosmo.

'Mr Baker, we need to take you down to the police station,' said the policeman. 'Your factory has been used for some time as a deposit and storage facility for the illegal export of ivory. Given the extensive and long-term nature of the operation, we have reasonable grounds to suspect that it was under your control.'

Father intervened: 'Hang on a moment. You can't suspect Cosmo. He is such a decent man. He could not possibly be involved in the export of ivory. You saw how those two devils had beaten him up. How could you suspect him?'

But his words had little impact on the police officers. They did not even respond.

Instead, the policewoman placed a hand on Uncle Cosmo's shoulder and said, 'Mr Cosmo Jeremy Baker, I'm arresting you for aiding and abetting the illegal procurement of ivory. I must warn you that anything you say or do may be recorded and used against you in evidence.'

Uncle Cosmo was silent. The brothers looked at each other, and Uncle Cosmo shook his head in disbelief.

The two police officers escorted him down the steps at the front of the house and into the waiting police car.

Josephine arrives at Wisteria House

As Uncle Cosmo left the house in a police car, Josephine was being released from the police station. She took a black cab to 17 Paradise Road. She could not wait to see Uncle Cosmo.

At Wisteria House everyone was still in a state of shock.

'I don't believe he was involved!' said Mother. 'Cosmo loves elephants. It would be completely out of character. Are you saying he has lost his moral compass?'

'No,' said Uncle Crispin. He was troubled. 'We've been told of this illegal operation taking place in his factory. If it had been going on for years, how could he not have known or suspected a thing?'

'We don't know what evidence the police have,' said Aunt Lily. 'But one would hope they would have searched for fingerprints on all the ivory and chocolate bars here and in the factory. Surely, if he is involved, his fingerprints will be all over the ivory.'

'Uncle Cosmo said that he knew everyone at the factory, and that they were like family,' said Tom.

'Could they not have run the operation at night?' questioned Johnny.

'Yes,' agreed Uncle Crispin. 'If they did, then I think it is completely plausible that Uncle Cosmo would not know about it. But there must be an inside team!'

'I hadn't thought of that,' said Father. 'It would

theoretically be possible for an illegal factory to operate at night. And Cosmo has always liked routine. I imagine he shuts up shop at 5 p.m. and opens the gates early the next morning. So the poachers could drop their haul in at night, and the ivory could be packaged and then posted the next morning. Cosmo would not have any reason to return at night-time.'

'So there would be no need to involve him in the operation,' observed Aunt Lily.

Rose piped up: 'Yes, and the link in all of this must be the secretary. She is the one who said, "Beware the Blackbird".'

The conversation was interrupted by Josephine knocking on the door. She had not met Cosmo's brothers and their wives, although she had seen them briefly when she was led into police custody. It was slightly awkward. She introduced herself again as Josephine Miller, and asked if Cosmo was there. Father invited her to come inside.

When she had had a cup of tea, Father had to tell her gently that Uncle Cosmo had been arrested that morning. He tried his best, but there is no gentle way to tell someone that the police have arrested the person you love. It was a shock. But the biggest shock was that the police now suspected that Cosmo had run the whole operation.

'Oh, no. He could not have done that. I am sure,' Josephine said, aghast. 'I am just so sure. Not Cosmo.'

She fiddled nervously with her hands. Unconsciously, she touched her bracelet. 'Elephants are such charismatic animals. They are the giants who rule the plains of Africa. Kindness makes kings and queens of them. Cosmo could not kill these regal creatures. Nor could he be involved in the export of their ivory!'

'Who could run this operation from the factory?' asked Rose gently.

'I just don't know,' said Josephine. 'I keep asking myself the same question.'

Hearing Josephine's sincerity, and concern, Mother and Father privately felt guilty for ever having imagined that she might have been behind the operation.

Time in Prison

Uncle Cosmo sat on the cold, hard bench of the prison cell. It was as if a light bulb were slowly going on in his head. He had first heard the rumours about a blackbird from his secretary Doris.

'Now, what about her uncle, Sir Reginald Ashurst?' he muttered under his breath. 'He could have done it. He often visited his niece at the factory in the late afternoon. He had a big black car. He was friendly, but formal. I found him a bit aloof with me, despite being a fairly regular visitor. I always thought he was just a doting uncle, because he often arrived laden with presents for his niece. He was a very successful businessman, with powerful political friends and was rumoured to own a Blackbird aeroplane. This was supposed to be a super-fast spy plane.'

At the time, Uncle Cosmo had thought it was only gossip. As far as he knew, no one had ever seen the plane. Now he sat and thought about it. He strained to remember the tale and its circumstances. He also recalled that the source of gossip was Plumb and Grimble, who had claimed to have flown in it!

When the police came to give him his lunch, he said, 'Ask Plumb and Grimble about the Blackbird. And ask them about Sir Reginald Ashurst. Plumb and Grimble bragged once about flying with him in his Blackbird aeroplane. No one ever saw it, and everyone suspected Plumb and Grimble of telling tall stories.'

The police guard nodded. Uncle Cosmo sat back with his plate. It had two slightly stiff slices of bread on it. His glass was full of tepid milk. He thought he could improve both the stale bread and warm milk by dipping the bread into the milk. As he slowly digested his meal, he recalled the moment when Doris had said, 'Beware the Blackbird'. He had scarcely heard her. She must have been frightened . . . perhaps she was scared that the phone was bugged and thought if she whispered she might not be overheard. Maybe her uncle was in the factory. Uncle Cosmo shuddered.

He suddenly recalled the moment before he fled: the moment when someone pointed a gun at him. The man was wearing a balaclava. He did not recognise him at the time. But what else was he wearing? Was it a suit? Could it have been Sir Reginald Ashurst? Or could the two men have been Plumb and Grimble? And why, at the very moment the masked men appeared, did his secretary give him his passport and a plane ticket?

The Dinner Party

That Saturday evening at an elegant home in Mayfair, London, owned by Sir William Silver, there was a grand dinner party with twenty-four guests. Sir William was the greatest silver merchant London had ever known. His table was finely laid: in the middle were the most detailed silver sailing ships, which appeared as a flotilla setting sail down the long table. Fifty tall candles in silver candlesticks were burning and their flickering light glowed against the shiny silver sides of the ships. The silver cutlery had been laid with immaculate precision. Fresh peonies crowned the table in bursts of pinks and whites.

The distinguished guests were seated. Among

them were the Marquis of Queensbury, the Duke and Duchess of Wellington, the crazy inventor Gertrude Walpole, rising politician Rachel Shipleigh, journalist Edward Townton, and fashionista Marlene Mangalesa. One of his guests was Sir Reginald Ashurst, the wealthy uncle of Uncle Cosmo's secretary, Doris.

There was a hum of good conversation. Quails' eggs, caviar and exotic tamarillo chutney were daintily presented. At that point the police knocked on the door. The butler answered, and ushered them through to the dining room.

An old gentleman was finishing his story about entering his favourite club, many years earlier, with a beautiful young French woman on his arm: 'The butler had politely explained that women wearing trousers were not permitted in the dining room of the club. She asked the butler politely to hold her bag, then slipped her trousers off, folded them, and handed them to the butler. "Please look after them – I'll need them later," she smiled, and walked through to the dining room!'

Sir Reginald Ashurst was roaring with laughter. Then he began to regale the table with the secret of Audley Square, and the lamppost outside Number 2, which has a little trapdoor at its side for spies to collect coded messages, when the police officer stepped forward to arrest him. The room fell silent.

'Sir Reginald Percival Ashurst?' the police officer said, as she placed a hand on his shoulder.

Sir Reginald looked up. The smile fell from his face. 'Yes,' he said.

'You are under arrest for the systematic exportation of ivory.' Sir Reginald said nothing. He was too clever to admit it. A keen observer might have seen a slight tilt of acknowledgement in his head, though he wore a neutral, almost innocent expression. But the police now had enough evidence.

Earlier that day, Patrick Plumb and George Grimble had given a further statement. Sir Reginald Percival Ashurst was indeed the Blackbird.

Sir William Silver stepped forward and spoke to the police officer directly. 'I say, could we not just sort this out. I can vouch for Reggie – I mean Sir Reginald. I have known him since school.'

'I am afraid that it is not a matter of someone vouching for his good character, sir,' replied the police officer as she started to cuff Sir Reginald Ashurst. He kept quiet. The humiliation was creeping over him like a thick fog. He realised the game was up. But his good friend supported him.

'Look here, wait one moment. It just could not be Sir Reginald. The man owns half of Africa. His family is hugely wealthy, you know. He would not, and *could* not, stoop to ivory trading. It's impossible,' declared Sir William Silver loudly.

But the police merely nodded as they led Sir Reginald Ashurst away. He said nothing. He kept a dignified silence to try to hide his utter disgrace.

After a further extensive investigation the police concluded that neither Cosmo nor Josephine had been involved. The whole illegal operation had indeed been run at night. An hour after sunset the doors of the factory would be opened by Plumb and Grimble. A night shift of illegal workers would arrive to package and disguise huge hauls of ivory. The ivory would be shipped the next day alongside the legitimate business of coffee and cocoa.

When Uncle Cosmo had announced that he would send his nieces and nephews a great chocolate treat, Plumb had had the ingenious idea of hiding a shipment of ivory in an identical box, to be shipped alongside the gift. Sir Reginald Ashurst was impressed – a whole tusk is worth far more than ivory pieces. His family fortunes had been faltering in recent years, and this would have been a timely source of funds. It was all but impossible to disguise and smuggle a whole tusk, let alone nine at once. When the two boxes were mixed up and the mistake was discovered, Plumb and Grimble scrambled to London to try to fix it. Sir Reginald Ashurst did not tolerate mistakes.

Some time later, Plumb and Grimble plea-bargained and gave evidence in exchange for a lighter sentence. Their evidence was against the Blackbird, the mastermind behind the smuggling: Sir Reginald

Ashurst. They also confirmed that Uncle Cosmo and Josephine were not involved in any way.

Uncle Cosmo's secretary Doris had suspected, and then known, what was going on. But she had been too frightened of the consequences to say a word to anyone. She agreed to testify for Uncle Cosmo, despite being very nervous about her uncle's reaction. She was given police protection to do so: the police kept her safe from her uncle and his bad business associates.

The Family Gathering

As soon as he was released from prison, Uncle Cosmo hurried back to Wisteria House. He swept Josephine up in his arms and gave her a big kiss. Then he thanked each of his nieces and nephews for all their help. It turned out that Sir Reginald Ashurst had been on the police suspect list for years. But they had never had enough evidence to arrest him, until now.

Everyone congregated in the kitchen to help prepare a family feast: Sunday lamb on a bed of rosemary. As they made a toast for Cosmo's safe return, the noise levels steadily rose to a pleasant pitch.

Over the laughter and joy at being reunited,

Rose's voice piped up with a serious question: 'Why would anyone want to kill an elephant?' The room quietened.

'The poachers want the ivory,' said Father.

Tom asked, 'Is it also because they are hungry that they kill the elephants – for their meat?'

'No, the main reason is for the ivory,' said Uncle Cosmo. 'The meat is just a by-product, and apparently pretty tough to eat. But they often dry it to make biltong. It's the ivory tusks that fetch thousands of pounds on the black market.'

'But who would buy ivory?' asked Bella.

'There is still a very strong market for it in Asia,' said Uncle Crispin. 'And I believe the United States is the world's second-largest market.'

'But why?' exclaimed Bella. 'The world is a much nicer place with more elephants and less jewellery.' She looked at Josephine and smiled. 'Sorry, Josephine.'

'Yes, it's true, the world would be better with more elephants,' said Josephine. 'But it's not just ivory. We all make choices when we buy things.'

'I agree,' said Uncle Cosmo. 'I love elephants.

I have read a lot about them over the years. You know, people have carved ivory for thousands of years. But the current problem started in earnest several hundred years ago when the plains of Africa still teemed with elephants. I have read that scientists and conservationists believe there were as many as twenty-six million.'

'What happened to all those elephants?' asked Rose.

'They were hunted for their tusks: the West wanted ivory for things like piano keys, white billiard balls, brushes, combs and ornaments,' said Uncle Cosmo.

'Ivory was a great luxury,' said Josephine.

'There has been an insatiable demand for ivory,' added Uncle Crispin.

'The desire for ivory was so strong that the elephant population more than halved over the nineteenth century,' said Uncle Cosmo. 'During the twentieth century the same trend continued until there were under a million elephants left. It was almost too late.'

'I remember when I first arrived in Africa I saw pictures on the news of Kenya burning its stores of ivory. This sent such a strong message to the world,' added Josephine, 'that a few months later, in 1989, there was a world ban on ivory poaching. The ban worked for about ten years. And the elephant population started to grow.'

'What happened next?' asked Rose.

'Well, two official sales of confiscated ivory tusks were allowed, which made it easier to trade in illegal ivory that was being passed off as legal,' said Uncle Cosmo. 'Now there are fewer than half a million elephants left in Africa.'

'Ivory is still a status symbol in parts of the world,' said Josephine. 'As Asia gets wealthier, the demand for it increases.'

Uncle Cosmo added: 'And once again the elephant population has started dropping at an alarming rate. They are likely to be extinct in the wild within ten years.'

'I've read it may only be six years,' said Father.

'Do you know that elephants live in family

groups, are highly intelligent and mourn the death of any member of the herd – just like us!' said Uncle Cosmo. 'Elephants cry; their eyes well with tears.'

'The Chinese translation for ivory is "elephant teeth",' said Josephine. 'This aids the misconception that tusks can fall out naturally.'

'Can they?' asked Tom.

'No,' said Uncle Cosmo. 'Only the baby tusks fall out after a year, and permanent ones replace them. Tusks continue to grow throughout an elephant's life. Poachers kill the elephants.'

'The killing of wildlife is also about the money,' said Josephine. 'The rhinoceros too are being killed for their horn. A sufficient number of people believe that it has a medicinal value. This has made rhino horn worth more than gold.'

Uncle Cosmo added: 'You know that rhino horn is made almost entirely of keratin, the same protein found in human hair, fingernails and toenails? There's a chap, name of Wilby, I believe, who sends his toenail clippings by post to the Chinese Embassy in Pretoria. He wants to emphasise the stupidity of killing rhino for keratin. Anyone could obtain this treasured keratin just by grinding up their own toe-nail clippings.'

'And it's free,' observed Freddie. 'And easy to find. Look!' he pointed at his own fingernails. 'They can have mine!'

'And mine!' shouted Tom.

'And mine!' chorused the other children.

When the room had quietened, Josephine drew the conversation back to ivory. 'Some Chinese people also believe that ivory protects against poison and that chopsticks will change colour when they come into contact with poisoned food.'

'Will ivory really change colour?' asked Rose.

'No,' said Josephine, shaking her head. 'But remember it is not so very long ago that we held similar views. In the National Museum of Scotland I've seen an old ivory book cover called Barbreck's Bone. The good people of Argyll used to believe it could cure madness.'

'Such a belief is madness!' said Bella. 'As if some piece of old ivory could cure anybody.'

'I hate ivory ornaments,' said Tom. 'They remind me that an elephant has died. I wish they would burn them all!'

'But that would not solve the problem,' said Father, 'and it would not bring the elephants back. The heat of the fire would not dry their tears.'

'The old ivory carvers in China do carve exquisitely,' observed Mother. 'It's such a shame they choose to use ivory. In her house in Paris, my Grandmother had exquisite Chinese woodcarvings and the way the light danced on the wood was extraordinary. I find it much more beautiful.'

'Wouldn't it be better', said Rose, 'to build a few large museums for all the ivory in the world. That way people could give their ivory to the museum.'

'To house all the ivory in the world, they would need to be elephantine museums!' said Johnny.

'I think that is a marvellous idea,' said Uncle Cosmo. 'It might really work, particularly if governments made it illegal to own ivory, but legal to donate it to a museum.'

'I agree,' said Josephine. 'I would happily give my

bracelet if it were illegal to own ivory.' She took off her bracelet. 'I will not wear this bracelet again. I now think it is right that only elephants should wear ivory.' Everyone agreed.

'I find it so odd that ivory can be a status symbol,' said Bella.

'My friends would think less of someone for supporting the killing of elephants,' said Johnny.

'Mine too,' said Freddie.

'It's so selfish to want to own ivory,' said Rose.

'Can people think of nothing better to compete for?' said Tom.

'I agree, Tom,' said Aunt Lily. 'I wish people would find something else as a status symbol. For example, during the Italian Renaissance rich Italians competed with each other over who had the most fabulous garden. The amazing water features and fountains used gravity and engineering feats so clever that they created gardens more stunning than any ivory ornament in the world!'

'If only people took more pride in gardening, if only . . .' mused Mother. Lucky barked. Socrates lay asleep on the windowsill of Wisteria House. The family smiled at each other and felt a quiet sense of relief for everyone's safe return. At the same time the children felt great sadness for the elephant herds whose families would not, like theirs, return.

For more information about how to
help the elephants please visit:

www.spaceforgiants.org
www.unitedforwildlife.org
www.sheldrickwildlifetrust.org
www.worldwildlife.org
www.elephantfamily.org
www.facebook.com/HandsOffOurElephants

For Zella's website visit
www.ladyzella.com

Acknowledgements

To my fabulous family, who have read this book and encouraged me. Thank you.

To my lovely friends and their amazing children who have read, listened and talked to me about this book. Thank you.

Special thanks also go to: Colin Thomann and Essie Cousins for wise counsel and guidance.

Pamela Thomann for editing services and interesting discussions about the power of the semi-colon, and the importance of language.

Silvia Crompton, Sylvia Kwan and Rachel Smyth for being such a fantastic professional team.

Mandii Pope for exquisitely executing the Book-Bench sculpture of *An Elephant for Breakfast*.

The Putney Exchange for sponsoring the Book-Bench in support of the National Literacy Trust's campaign of books about town.

Tom Brunner: one brave day I telephoned him out of the blue and he was very encouraging about my book and how it might perhaps one day help elephants. He is a trustee for www.spaceforgiants.co.uk

Coming soon:

Another brave adventure,
set in London and Africa:
with a diamond tiara,
a wedding and a giraffe
for breakfast.

Lightning Source UK Ltd.
Milton Keynes UK
UKOW07f0834031114

240994UK00009B/36/P